THE SOMETIMES LAKE

THE SOMETIMES LAKE

SANDY BONNY

thistledown press

Thistledown Press Ltd.
118 - 20th Street West
Saskatoon, Saskatchewan, S7M 0W6
www.thistledownpress.com

Library and Archives Canada Cataloguing in Publication

Bonny, Sandra Marie, 1978-
The sometimes lake / Sandy Bonny.

Short stories.
Issued also in an electronic format.
ISBN 978-1-897235-99-7

I. Title.

PS8603.O62S66 2012   C813'.6   C2012-901130-4

Cover and book design by Jackie Forrie
Printed and bound in Canada

Canada Council   Conseil des Arts   SASKATCHEWAN   Canadian   Patrimoine
for the Arts   du Canada   ARTS BOARD   Heritage   canadien

Thistledown Press gratefully acknowledges the financial assistance of the Canada Council for the Arts, the Saskatchewan Arts Board, and the Government of Canada through the Canada Book Fund for its publishing program.

Acknowledgments

This collection was written over a number of years, in a number of cities, and has been blessed by the responses, perspectives, and enthusiasms of many, many friends and family. I feel very lucky and am very grateful.

Jeffy Baker (*nichewakan*), you have been an excellently nonsense-proof sounding board — with Ena, Julius, and Evelyn, thank you so much for your love and patience.

Mom (Sheila Bonny) and Meera Kachroo, thank you for your honesty and encouragement in your common role as first readers of early drafts.

Momentum for this project came from many quarters, but I would especially like to thank Lynn Coady for her mentorship through the Wired Writing Studio at the Banff Centre for the Arts, and David Carpenter and Jan Zwicky for their encouragement and confidence in my writing.

Many of these stories have appeared elsewhere (in slightly different form) and they have benefited in each instance from the guidance of journal editors.

All of these stories have benefited from prompts towards clarity and fluency from their final editor, Elizabeth Phillips — a big thank-you for your attentive-and-persistent-assistance.

Finally, thank you to Thistledown Press for bringing this collection to publication, and to the Alberta Foundation for the Arts and the Canada Council for the Arts for their support of my creative efforts.

Contents

. . . where the spirits meet the humans, the water meets the land, the child meets the adult—these are the zones of power, and I think this is really where stories are created.
— *Chinua Achebe*

Nògha

JENS FINDS HIMSELF DESCENDING IN A small and crowded plane. At sixty-three degrees latitude, he is just two degrees shy of the Arctic Circle. Which, arriving, he pictures as an actual circle. A bounded wilderness of ice and polar bears and muskoxen against which the school's painted aluminum roof will stand out — bright lichen orange beside the *National Geographic*'s tundra grey. The buildings that the plane coasts over are obscured by exhaust rising from idling vehicles at the side of the runway. It billows across a patchwork of gravel and snow.

After the three-hour flight, Jens needs a bathroom. Coming out, he finds that the other passengers have disappeared. The terminal is empty except for this woman, in pressed slacks and a plaid jacket, who knows exactly who he is.

"Jens Hill."

"Yens," he corrects, nodding.

"Right," she says, "I'm Joanne, with the school. The social worker." She copies Jens' nod and points him outside. She asks where he's from and when he says Vancouver, she smiles and says, "get used to flat." Flat and quiet and dirty brown at the tail end of winter. The airport control tower and the radio tower down the street are the tallest things in town, and almost level. Jens is looking between them when Joanne starts her truck. Blowing into his hands to warm them as she begins to tell him about the school.

Concrete brick construction on a raised foundation. Not well-insulated. Jacks at the corners to level the floors after the spring thaw, usually in later June. He could expect a crooked classroom. A school on shifting ground, windows screened to keep the black flies out at the back-to-school end of summer.

Joanne leads Jens down a fluorescent corridor tiered by wooden cubbyholes, each well-stuffed with boots and mittens. A buzzer sounds as they reach the office and they duck in, narrowly escaping a scuffle and squash of freed children. Jens is greeted by Nancy, the school secretary, who tosses him a fistful of keys and invites him to a get-together. Tonight. Some teachers and support staff, probably some of the environmental resource guys who work with her husband. Nothing fancy, a good way to meet everybody. Does it sound good?

"It sounds good," Jens agrees, turning to check with Joanne who has backed into the hallway to wave some children out. Behind Nancy, the vice-principal's

head pokes around the door of an inner office. He was friendly on the phone but seems distracted now, beckoning Jens into his office with one hand, bracing the other against the door frame.

Sitting opposite the vice-principal, Jens feels landed for the first time. He talks about his internship, telling the VP that he may not be the world's best teacher yet but he does really like teaching, engaging with his students. He found that they learned best when they came up with their own questions to explore. Their own science fair projects. His favourite, and one of the best projects in the end, was organized by a team of girls who studied cat sociology by introducing neighbourhood cats to one another in neutral territory versus inside one another's homes. There was another project on solar energy, kids who powered a shop fan using magnifying glasses to concentrate heat.

The VP leans across his desk and says, "There's not a lot of cats up here, the dogs eat them." He advises Jens that whole-group projects will be better suited to the students in this school. Attendance isn't great. English isn't strong. Parental support is limited. There is a curriculum but Mrs. Powell has managed the vital bits. Jens shouldn't stress himself over content coverage. Course materials can be ordered in but take three to six weeks to arrive and Jens has only seven weeks left in the term. The VP produces a stack of books and pamphlets and generously tells Jens he can "have at them." The focus is science, he adds, smiling finally, just "keep your class interested and *in order*." Chewing gum, truancy, and lice were what he'd warned Jens about on the phone.

The classroom Nancy leads Jens to looks like any grade seven space anywhere. Three rows of six desks, each a little crooked. Cream-coloured industrial lino with green and brown streaks. Narrow windows along one side of the room. Orange bulletin boards on the other, decorated by assignments, art, and seasonal cutouts.

Supervised by the school janitor, Martha, the students have spent the first three days of their science module producing a giant Mercator projection of the Earth. The continents are painted over a too dark shade of blue, so the ocean seeps up through Asia's orange edges and Antarctica's white. North America is a little off, stretched upwards by the curved lens of the overhead projector they used to trace its outline. And the Arctic islands are choppy, painted at the end of someone's outstretched arm. Canada is a shaky lime green land, squeezed out of the pole, with a tidy red star to mark the place where this school fits into the world.

Nancy tours Jens around the rest of the halls and common rooms, then leaves him with Barry, the senior phys. ed. instructor and RCMP liaison, who sketches the town for Jens on the back of a gym deferral slip. A five-by-seven block grid with messy circles showing Barry's place, Nancy's place, the school, the Co-op and Northern stores, and the condo-unit they've leased for Jens.

The condos are mini-duplexes. Eight in a row, with uniform brown plank siding. Jens' is at the far end of the row. Waving to Barry's truck, its trail of white exhaust, Jens fumbles through his new key ring and hears laughter in the suite beside his. On the drive over, between the school and the condos, Jens saw no one at all. Though the piles of dirty snow bordering the road were well trampled, he did not see a single person on the street. Not even kids meandering home. But there are a lot of people at his neighbour's. All talking together, laughing loudly, a TGIF well under way. Next to this, Jens' suite is large and empty. Two bedrooms and way more creaky square footage than he and his bags will fill. A first order of groceries has been provided — milk, sandwich meat, cheese and eggs, cereal, bread, peanut butter, pasta, and tomato sauce — still bagged in the fridge. And there are dishes, utensils, and pots and pans stacked beside the sink. Jens pulls a bag of ripple chips out of his duffel bag and settles himself on the living room couch. He pauses several times between crunches, listens, tries to pick phrases out through the wall, and can't.

By nine his neighbour's party is louder and Jens, showered and boots on, is desperate for company. Barry's instructions lead him past the town's ten streetlights. They have not yet flickered on, but the twilight is washed pale by a floodlight in the empty parking lot of the Northern store. Town really is flat, Jens finds. And incredibly quiet. So Jens hears the party before he sees Nancy's house, unmistakable as the only stuccoed one in town. A poor siding choice that, strained by water wedging itself into ice, has spalled pink flakes into the snow sagging around it. Jens follows a path of tramped snow down the side of the house and finds himself barred from this party by a spring-latched gate in a chain link fence that is easily two metres tall.

"We have small dogs!" Nancy shouts, scurrying over to let Jens in. They need the fence to keep the big dogs out, she explains. Big dogs and yes, sometimes cougars. Sure, the odd bear. Not wolves though, not this far from the mountains. Nancy re-latches the gate spring, then stoops to Jens' knees. She smiles up at him and pops a can of beer out of the snow banked up against her house. "Or you could wait a minute," she says, "if you need it colder?"

Jens takes the can. He clasps the beer between his mittens while Nancy rises and points out her husband, a bald head bobbing above the raised lid of their barbeque. She points across the yard, "And you know Joanne, don't you?" Jens nods, yes. Joanne, wearing the same outfit as earlier, is perched on the rail of Nancy's porch next to a man who is leaning into her, waving a fork. They are the only people not looking over at him. The only two in the yard who don't swarm in with introductions and welcomings.

Two hours and a belly full of grilled caribou later, Jens is on his knees, mining the pink stucco-flecked snow for remaining beer. The party has risen in volume and he finds himself shouting a warning to a resource technician intent on recruiting him to a basketball team, "I haven't played in years!"

"Babies," an older boy translates for him. "They want to learn what's wrong with Mrs. Powell's baby."

"Oh," Jens says, "Really? Right." He imagined they would want to learn about electricity, or computers, or geology — fossils and mountain building, volcanoes and climate change. He imagined they would know whatever they wanted to know about babies by grade seven. Only five of his students are actually eleven or twelve years old; three have been held back for language skills, three started late or failed earlier grades. Stacey, afternoons only, is twenty-two.

The ten-year age span made the *interesting* part of *in order* tricky. The VP had suggested a democratic learning model. Let them vote on the subject material. If they'd chosen electricity, Jens had a pickle in brine he could set up to glow. For geology he had a magic sinking ice cube routine. Babies stumped him.

"Spina bifida," Joanne said, was the problem with their teacher's baby, when Jens tracked her down over lunch. "She's having neonatal surgery."

Jens had only been told maternity leave. He had cheerfully promised to teach his students anything they wanted to know about and wasn't sure spina bifida could be stretched into a four-week module. Should he do a whole unit on human reproduction? Was there a community health nurse he could bring in?

"Oh, they know where babies come from," Joanne laughed, then coughed through a mouthful of sandwich. "Stacey has two at home. Hmm, and Darren has two in the oven, two ovens."

Jens nodded, "Well, maybe we'll do climate change then . . ."

Joanne swallowed. "Jens, if you seriously told them they could decide then you have to do what they picked. We're trying to emphasize accountability around here. But forget Mrs. Powell's baby. If you're going to teach them about babies, teach them how to grow them right. Show them what booze and drugs will do."

Jens disappoints his class with a chalkboard demonstration of bacterial division. One bacteria splits into two, then four, eight — then his chalk circles branched down through ellipses. This is growth, reproduction, and he tells them that it's amazing. Thousands of 'babies' could be made overnight.

"We're lucky not everything grows as quickly as bacteria, aren't we? Did you know that there are almost seven billion people on Earth? That's seven thousand million! So . . . if each person on Earth right now had two children, and nobody died, how many people would there be?" Jens calculates this with algebra, 'X' = (2 x Y) + Y, 'Y'= 7 billion people, so 'X' = (2 x 7 billion people) + 7 billion people = 21 billion people!

"Neat, isn't it?" he asks, then, "have you seen this kind of math before?"

The younger kids are staring at him. The older ones are looking out the window, or at their desks. In the front row thirteen-year-old Nathan is busy filling the white Nike swoosh on his sneaker in with ballpoint cross hatching. At the back, Stacey looks up from a notebook, blinks at the board, and shakes her head, No.

"It went great," He tells his mom on the phone. And really, the class hadn't been that disruptive or disrespectful. They did seem a little tired and bored. The math was over their heads and nobody had raised a hand to interrupt him. Also, during morning reading time the youngest ones pushed their desks together at the back of the room and whispered in quick, quiet Dene Tha' that Jens cannot understand. He knows '*Ts'ido*' is children. And has learned that '*Nògha*' is 'Wolverine' because X-men 3 is playing on the pull-down screen at the library. The grades one to three boys shout "*Snikt!*" on the playground, popping their fists open and springing their fingers out to imitate Wolverine's metallic claws. "*Snikt,*" dramatic pause, "*Nògha!*" Then a theatrical howl. Jens told his students that if they didn't feel like reading or listening they could put their heads on their desks and rest, which prompted a ten-minute class-wide nap.

Jens pulls out his classroom management course notes on his mom's advice. He digs out the VP's pamphlet on culturally inclusive curricula and falls promptly asleep inside it. He dreams that he is shouting from the front of his classroom, slamming his palms down on the demonstration table, trying and trying to keep his students awake. They slouch in their desks, unbelievably skinny and drowning in track pants and hoodies three times their size. Smooth black-haired heads rise up from puddles of black clothing — the fashion hand-me-downs of rappas and gangstas. In Jens' dream his students ask him for 'bling'.

"Okay. We all know different things that grow. Can anyone give me an example?"

Quiet.

Quiet.

Someone farts. Shirts are pulled quickly up over noses. This seems to be the students' routine. No giggling. No smiles. Dry, necessary sensory self-defense.

"Okay," Jens says again. "I'm sure you've all planted seeds before?"

"Okay. We're going to plant some today."

They gather to watch Jens as he lays paper towel on a tray. He commandeers Judie to set out two little rows of bean seeds between layers of paper towel, then tries to get the rest involved, arming sixteen-year-old Darren with a spray bottle to wet the towel. The other kids hang back, avoiding the mist. Beans planted, they shuffle back to their clustered desks to label and colour a seedling diagram that Jens has downloaded. There's no Dene word for cotyledon, the bilingual kids point out, just 'leaf'. "That's interesting," Jens says. They squeak their shoes against the lino under their desks, antsy for the two o'clock bell. They are being dismissed early because of a staff meeting.

Jens stands in the door of the class and waves "Bye, see you tomorrow, have a good afternoon," and only then does tiny Esther, who has not made a noise all day, pause in the hall to tell him that when they grew beans last year they put the seeds in organic cotton batting, not paper towel, because some paper towel has bleach in it that will make the seeds not grow. He thanks her, closes the classroom door, and straightens their desks into rows.

Jens finds coffee and Joanne in the staff room. He's early for the meeting, the coffee is overbrewed, and Joanne is busily clearing mouldy food out of the shared fridge. Not exactly her job description, Jens thinks, but things that get shoved to the back of the fridge get too cold and freeze, then get shuffled forward and rot.

"Yuck," he agrees. "Hey, Joanne, do you know how Mrs. Powell is doing?"

"Ready to leave already?" she asks, her face turned down to a crisper drawer.

Jens shakes his head. "My kids were asking about her."

Joanne jerks her head out of the fridge, "They're not your kids, Jens. They're not even kids, most of them — they're your students."

Jens blinks and Joanne slams a rancid looking sandwich bag into the garbage pail. "What?" she asks, glaring up at him, "Didn't they teach you that at teacher school?"

Late in the meeting, they learn that a favourite student from the last community Joanne worked in has killed herself. She announces this after the VP holds up a poster made by the grade twos for a visiting elder. It is colourful and crafty, but their teacher wrote *Thank you for coming to tell us about caribou worms, sorry for not sitting and listening quietly* across the top, and left a space for all the kids to sign. The VP wants less apologetic thank-you's after pre-K literary skills week. Jens tries to be interested and attentive, but pre-K literary skills week won't involve his class. His coffee is bitter and he sets his cup down on the table. He considers mentioning that his class is too quiet, that they need lessons in speaking up.

But, thoughts turned to his potentially poisoned beans, Jens waives his turn to speak, leaving the floor open for Joanne to announce that all the reading skills in the world won't do anyone any good if the students are dead. That they should be getting the elders in to talk about traditional values, not reinforcing colonial knowledge systems. That Jacey Modeste, the girl who won the Northern Math Olympiad at Radio Lake, swallowed two bottles of aspirin and died of pulmonary edema. That Jacey did this over her lunch break.

The VP sighs, shakes his head, and points out that they haven't had a suicide at his school for more than five years. "You worked in Radio Lake, didn't you Joanne? Was she a favourite student?"

You shouldn't have favourites, Jens catches himself thinking. Didn't they teach her that in social worker school?

Jens is at school until eight that night, making up a poster with Celsius to Fahrenheit conversions and using the internet terminal in the 'library' — a row of four bookshelves in the corner of the African animal-themed kindergarten/first grade classroom. There is a larger town library for the teachers and high school students but Jens prefers Google to reference texts tonight. He likes the hollow feeling the school has after hours. The solemn rumble and hum of Martha's vacuum moving through the halls. He learns that the brand of paper towel he scavenged from the teacher's bathroom does not contain bleach. And that Radio Lake, five degrees north, is well within the Arctic Circle and probably still has snow. Here it has mostly disappeared and he has been walking to and from school over the sharp edges of frozen mud, footprinted and tire-tracked in the brief midday thaw. The rounded conversion from Fahrenheit to Celsius given by ConversionsOnline, $T_f = (9/5){}^*T_c)+32$, will be a good one to use to introduce his class to calculators and equivalent equations, not to mention temperature. Jens has decided that their group project will be to build a therma-stable incubator and grow chickens.

The older boys build the incubator, taking an extra afternoon with the Industrial Arts teacher to frame and glaze a two- by four-foot crate. Stacey's husband, an electrician, helps them set up wiring to connect the heat lamp to a self-adjusting thermostat. "It's good, it's really good," Jens tells them. Miles better than the plans he downloaded. This incubator even has a spinning tilted tray to rotate the eggs, courtesy of someone's father.

Nine of Jens' twelve students come Friday morning to see the eggs placed in their wire stand, and seven stay after lunch to start on the posters of chicken fetal development. They work in groups of two and three, illustrating the stages of growth. Drawing tattoos in ballpoint pen rapidly becomes more interesting than chicken embryos to the younger students. The noise level in the next class rises, and Jen's three youngest girls, Esther, Judie, and Mina, start shrieking, daring each other to smell the markers, shoving them at each others' noses. The teenage boys, sprawled on the floor, impede Jens' progress towards what is threatening to develop into a full-blown marker fight and he shouts, "Girls!" "*Ts'ido!*" But Stacey reaches them first and drags a protesting Judie out of the classroom to wash a green streak off her cheek. At three o'clock Stacey is suddenly also gone and at three-fifteen the bell leaves Jens waving "Bye" from a sea of scattered paper and shoved-aside desks.

At the end of the week, Jens is in the VP's office. Trying not to be obvious about asking for help, he asks instead how his class behaved for Mrs. Powell.

"Great," the VP smiles. "She's a bitch."

And for Martha, when they made the poster of Earth?

"Well, she's Judie's grandma."

Jens nods.

The VP opens his hands, drops his pen onto the desk. "They know better than to sass an old lady in braids."

The pilot who brought the eggs from a hatchery in Yellowknife, along with a load of tarpaper, said he was up from Michigan to make some cash. He said his name was Dan, just Dan.

"How d'you like 'em?" he asked Jens.

"They're all right, good thanks," Jens answered, worried about the temperature in the box of eggs that Dan had held out to him in wintry air.

"You know why they all go to church on Sunday, hey?"

"Why's that?" Jens asked, distracted, trying to fit the box beneath the open flap of his coat.

"If they kneel down to pray they get a look up Virgin Mary's skirt."

"Right," Jens smiled. The people. The town. Not the eggs. Eggs going to church on Sunday, though, that was a funny idea.

Every single egg survives. Tuesday morning, Jens candles them with the students to see the embryos' stage of development. Books and posters set aside for the afternoon, he herds them into library to compare their observations with an online database of 'chicken development'. At five days past fertilization the embryos they saw looking like bean seeds, suspended in spidery blood vessels, have beating hearts, spinal cords, eyes, and nubs that will be wings and feet.

"Look up what's wrong with our teacher's baby for them," Stacey says. So Jens does. He searches for pictures of children with spina bifida and finds them grinning up from tiny walkers. He finds a web page that explains how neonatal surgery is risky but can help. There is a picture of a fetus reaching out of its womb to grab a surgeon's finger. "Did she have that operation yet?" they want to know.

"Yes." Jens tells them. He has heard that much through the other teachers. "Mrs. Powell is doing really well," he says, knowing nothing of the details.

"She's coming back up here soon, then?" Nathan asks. He is frowning over the caterpillar of his first mustache at the fetus's tiny fingers, and Jens finds himself embarrassed suddenly by the pink balloon of the woman's womb.

Stacey answers, "After that baby is actually born."

"Probably in the summer," Jens agrees. "Should we look up something else?"

Jens tries again. "Does anyone have something else they'd like to look up?"

The students are pointing and whispering over the fetal hand. They are speaking half in Dene and Jens is about to call them to order when someone coughs out, "Wolverine." Scanning his students' suddenly quiet faces, Jens is not sure who asked, but raises his eyebrows and turns back to the computer. He types 'Wolverine' and gets almost equal hits for Hugh Jackman's X-man and Hinterland Who's Who sites. The tenth hit is for Nògha, a Dene prophet.

"Do you guys know about this guy?" Jens asks, interested to have stumbled into cultural content. But, yeah, yeah, the students nod.

Yeah, yeah, Stacey nods too. She puffs out her cheeks, points up the list, "Click on that one." Hugh Jackman's leather-bound muscles slouched in a doorway. Lips pouted, eyes sulking. Wolverine at Marvel Universe. The kids nod, puff out their cheeks. Judie, squinting at Wolverine's claws, slips the end of her ponytail into her mouth and chews.

Maybe it's not science, but at least they can practise literary skills. Jens lets them take turns sitting in front of the computer to read Wolverine's biography out loud. Wolverine is Canadian, they learn, from Alberta. He is a mutant orphan who watched his dad get murdered and his mom kill herself. He goes by Logan, but his real name is James Howlett. His claws are made of a mineral, adamantium, not metal. He's proud, and his temper gets him into trouble. But he has also has keen animal senses and can heal from anything, death included. Same as Wolverine, Nògha, the trickster. Logan married an Indian named Silver Fox. And then after she got murdered he avenged her by fighting the Wendigo — the people who eat people.

But, "No," Jens tells the students, he doesn't think Wolverine is supposed to be Indian. And the story isn't scientifically true. People can't really be mutants. Do they know if wolverines really howl the way Logan does in the movie? The way you'd expect someone named *Howlett* to howl?

"No," Judie snorts. "Wolverines squeak and hiss."

"Like a badger," Stacey explains, smiling.

But Jens hasn't heard a badger.

"Like a shot badger," Nathan amends, which Jens has also never heard.

"Like this," Esther demonstrates, "Hssssssssssssssrrrrrrrrrrrrrr . . . *Snikt!*" Fingers clicking open as bright adamantine claws. The howling, she assures Jens, is just for the movies.

Jens follows Joanne's advice with the bean plants. After the seeds have sprouted, he transfers them into potting soil and divides the pots into two rows. He dispenses four shots of vodka into a one-litre beaker, tops it off with water and pours it over the first row of plants. The other row gets tap water, dumped unceremoniously by James, a grudging volunteer. Each student writes the details of the method and an experimental hypothesis into their science notebook. Then they watch Jens lock the bottle of Russian Prince in the chemical cabinet at the back of the room. He finds himself nervous, keeping his hands busy with photocopies, until the silence is broken by a giggle. A fart. A yelp as somebody hits somebody else.

"Okay," he says, clapping. Clapping louder, "Grade sevens!"

Jens wakes to the bang of an ice raft cracking in the river and pictures it spinning apart in the current. He has dreamt of hatched chicks, hundreds of them, running amok between his legs. But the eggs are cold when he reaches in to turn the tray in the incubator at the front of his classroom that morning. The heat lamp is on and humming, and the air inside it is warm. Jens lifts an egg and sees a stamp on the side of it. A small red circle that he knows from the eggs in his refrigerator as the inventory brand the Co-op uses. He hears Martha shuffling before he sees her standing with a garbage can near the back of the room.

"Guess you shouldn't put booze in there," she says, pointing to the chemical cabinet, which is listing off the wall behind her. They have broken the lock, scattered salts and magnesium ribbon around the back of the room. The Russian Prince is gone.

Jens looks over to the bean seedlings by the back window, but no one has touched their tray. The yellow fetal alcohol ones are stunted but whole, twisting up beneath the long green stalks of the healthy beans.

"I found some more eggs," Martha says.

Jens nods. They frown at each other.

"I cleaned up the broke ones," she says. She holds out her garbage pail and in it Jens can see eggshells and, pushing them aside with his finger, the small curled bodies of what would have been chickens, beaks and feathers well started. Jens is not sure if

Martha knows that, besides talking about them constantly, her granddaughter had each of those chickens named.

"I set those eggs up all right in there," Martha asks.

"Thank you," Jens says. "Thanks, Martha."

He unplugs the incubator after she leaves.

Jens examines the chemical cabinet and manages to set it right on the wall, though it won't quite latch. It has been kicked or punched open, he thinks. And they've taken his baking soda and a bar of soap and the jar of sugar crystals precipitated with food colouring that Mrs. Powell made to talk about minerals. Jens had planned to pull it out and talk about adamantine, a grey kind of sapphire that Marvel claims is resistant to metal-munching bacteria. He was going to talk about whether there was any science behind that and thinks that he still might because even without props it could be a distraction from the eggs. And from Mrs. Powell and her baby who the kids keep asking about. As if Jens should know how this woman, who he has never even met, and her child, who has not yet been born, are doing at all times. As if teachers are part of a secret society and know everything about each other the way the students seem to know everything about each other. "Mrs. Powell's doing well," Jens tells them. He repeats this, day after day, because this is all he's heard in the staff room since Joanne stopped joining the rest of them at lunch.

Before the morning bell, in the gap that Jens usually uses to check his email, he finds himself in the staff washroom, rubbing the Co-op stamps off the eggs with an unbleached paper towel. When the students show up, seven that day, the incubator is plugged back in, the eggs are warm, and Jens has managed to jam the cabinet door closed with a paper clip.

At morning recess there is a fight amongst the grade nines over something no one will explain to the teachers, and Nathan and

James have blood on their T-shirts when they come back to class. Jens spends lunch in Joanne's office. He goes by to see why she hadn't been over to Nancy's on the weekend and ends up listening to her rant about students stealing money and smokes from the 'locked' staff room closet.

She leans toward him, whispering because the walls are thin. "Someone around here is too chickenshit to report a lost key." She is sick, she says, of the shit being pulled around this school. Jens offers her half a cookie as consolation but by afternoon recess the stolen smokes have been passed around and a girl burns her younger brother's cheek with one of them. The vice-principal locks the school doors and lectures the students in the gravel playground about *Respect* and *Just Say No* before he lets them back in. Jens watches the lecture through the grid wire shatterproof glass of his classroom windows. The students' faces are scrunched, loud in silent 'it wasn't me, these aren't my problems'. Most of the kids have taken off to go home. It's pretty well guaranteed that none of the stragglers left in schoolyard stole anything or attacked anyone during the recess break. In lipstick, on the back of the gym door, someone was busy writing *So Fuken What!*

The fifth weekend in town, the fifth Sunday that Jens wakes up hungover from a teacher-resource staff get-together, his sleep is foiled by crashing and laughter in his neighbours' unit. Louison, Nell, their three grown children, and their handfuls of grandchildren never seem to leave or sleep for long. They were up when Jens flopped into bed, having dragged himself home through a night as bright as afternoon. They are up now, in a morning light that also feels afternoonish. Down south, Jens has learned. 'Yanaghé,' south. Down south there is still night and the cities are anonymous and teachers drink in bars, not fenced yards and basements.

The morning Jens wakes up to is dimmed by aerosols drifting in from Alaska where a forest is burning — miles and miles of destructive heat and flame. Here the smoke dampens everything. The sun is dull, with the faint red glow of a candled egg. A candled unfertilized egg. Jens has been raised never to look directly at the sun. Not during an eclipse, not through a cloud, not ever. Now, listening to a ruckus through the wall, the shriek and running feet of a child being dressed, Jens stares straight at a sun whose circumference strikes him as disturbingly small. And coinike. Copper red. And suddenly that sun is eclipsed by Louison and Nell, clumping close past Jens's window with a string of children and grandchildren, bundled against the chill and headed to church.

Jens has walked past but not into the church. His first week in town he decided to go and see the dogs, the trained ones that were kept just beyond the church's yard of white crosses. With the snow already too wet for sleds, the dogs were tethered in a pound. Each dog had a rope around its neck tied to a peg driven into the frozen mud beside its boxy doghouse. The dogs were shaggy, shedding, and sat up when he came near the fence, floppy ears up and white blue and brown eyes expectant. Jens had nothing to throw them. Didn't know their names and was afraid to pet them. They seemed to know that he didn't know what to do and rose barking. Howling. Climbing on top of their houses to howl louder. Jens hurried away, embarrassed to have started them up — but he's heard them many times since. They bark at the garbage trailer. At four wheelers. At kids running over to rattle their fence after Sunday school.

Tuesday evening, Dan flies up unscheduled. He comes to transport a man who treated his wife worse than her brothers would put up with down to a hospital in Edmonton. He has also brought a delivery and Jens is called to the airstrip from the school where he has been busy on the computer again, looking for job postings in lower mainland BC. Mrs. Powell really is okay, Jens has heard, finally. Her baby will probably be okay too, Nancy said, and her husband will be the at-home parent so Mrs. Powell plans to be back teaching by September. This makes Jens feel better about leaving, though the district principal and VP have indicated they could find him a class if he wanted to stay in the North.

At the side of the gravel runway, pilot Dan leans in to Jens with smoky breath, and gesturing at the beaten man whose wife is climbing into the plane beside him, whispers, "We might as well cage 'em in and give 'em knives, eh? Finish 'em off."

Jens blushes but can't voice a reply. He doesn't know at this point that he will never forget the joke. That is won't fade away like other details, like most of his students' names or the dimensions of his classroom. And because he doesn't know this, Jens turns quickly, thanking Dan for the delivery. The hatchery in Yellowknife has sent a dozen freshly hatched chicks with an invoice slip *Attn: Mr. Hill.* They are scratching and peeping inside a perforated shoebox. They are a few days premature for the twenty-one days of incubation, but Jens doesn't think his students will mind, or maybe notice. He might adjust the countdown on the board a little, to fit. Next to the board, there's a poster the kids made that says *Elephant, eighteen to twenty-four months; Woman, nine months; Chicken, twenty-one days; Mouse, eighteen days.* There aren't enough days left in the term to breed the mice that Esther has set her heart on so Jens has told her to ask her teacher for a mouse project in the fall. For now, he is sure his kids are going to love these airmail chickens.

There's a new problem, though. Either Martha asked for too many when she called the order in or the hatchery decided to be generous. Probably the latter. Jens can imagine Martha on the phone, telling whoever was on the other end how excited her Judie was to see brand-new hatched chickens. How Judie couldn't stop talking about them. How vodka-stealing idiots weren't going to get their way disappointing her granddaughter. No way, no how. Not after that little girl had every single egg already named. Well, Martha wouldn't get that dramatic. Probably she just said she needed some chicks. Ten of them. Please and thank you. For Mr. Hill. Then whoever filled the box counted out twelve.

Either way, a full dozen chickens means that the ten Co-op eggs Jens has kept at stubbornly stable temperature in the front corner of his classroom will have to miraculously hatch two sets of twins. And checking the invoice again, he notices that the hatchery has also sent a turkey. Eleven chickens, one turkey.

Peering into the box, Jens thinks the turkey is this one, which is larger, and ganglier, with a few tan brown feathers on its fluffy wings. He picks it up and sees that its egg tooth is still attached, a raised pearl on its tiny beak. Its legs kick and grab at Jens's wrists, moving sticks with surprisingly sharp claws. When he lowers it into the incubator the turkey twists and drives, stabbing at the thumb ring that he wears on his right hand. Jens has never seen anything like it.

Frames

IF YOU DON'T LEAVE YOUR MIND open, you're not going to see them. You're not going to see them through a telescope, either. The field of view is too small. That was how it started. The two of us packing up cheese and a spiked thermos and going out to sit on a sleeping bag, dark nights, midsummer.

I said, "Night is quite another world from the day." Cooler, all the cars or most of the cars on the highway gone to sleep, and while other people sat out on their porches with bug lights and Kaiser decks, Megan and I went out on the fields, past the suburban houses and the sewage treatment plant and the half-sculpted golf course and we spread my sleeping bag out, slippery side down, felt side up, and watched the sky for alien space ships.

Megan brought a headlamp and she switched it on, an hour in, to do some reading by. I sat at the edge of its light and tried to focus my eyes on the dark heads waving around us. Horsetails, wild oats. Thistles routed out. What lived there bent in the breeze, quick and green-painted-blue by the night.

By the end of the summer the grass didn't bend. It waved stiff and rustled around me looking up, and Megan happy to read in the shuffled quiet.

Dark nights, no moon nights, with grasshoppers chirping, we could see, away from the city, the spilled salt of the Milky Way. The tipped cup of stars falling through the satellites.

Megan said the Milky Way didn't spill, it condensed. And the stars aren't falling, because every little bit of the universe is expanding. It has been for a while, everywhere. And "that is not a satellite, Stephanie, it's a plane."

I saw the black of Megan's eyes, inside the blue irises turned green by her headlamp. I heard her knowing things. I told her about a walk we took to the beach at night, Andrew and me, twelve years or so ago. After his family moved to Nanaimo and my mom finally broke down and paid for me to visit. It was grade ten, I think.

Andrew tried to skip a rock and lost it in the ocean. He threw a chunk of scrap wood in next and it splashed out away from us, sending up sparkles. Haloes of yellowy green in the water. Not reflected off the water, but in the water. Glowing water. I saw magic and didn't want to be tricked.

"Look at that!" Andrew said, pointing to the edge of the circles rippling out from the log, the edge where the glow diffused. He was pleased.

I imagined glow-in-the-dark water powder. Something that could be opened and poured over a piece of scrap wood, like the packet that turned my mom's tea to solid jelly. Stiffum's Powder that my uncle brought home from a business trip. It smelled like turpentine and the tea looked like congealed bacon fat by the time the reaction finished. I had wanted to keep my mom from lifting the cup to her mouth but my uncle said, wait, let's see what she'll do.

"Nice," I said, on the beach.

"Nice, Andrew." I wanted to turn his hands over and see if there was some residue, if his hands were glowing too. But Andrew didn't like being touched, and he looked happy for once. We walked back to his mom's house and drank his dad's beer.

"How long are you thinking we'll wait tonight?" Megan asked, an hour into our third trip to not see UFOs.

I told her, "I'm a very patient person," which isn't quite true.

"Check out that tree." I pointed to a tree-shaped silhouette across the field. I thought she'd like that. I thought she'd tell me what kind of tree it was.

She nodded.

I had Megan by moonlight, crouched and twisting my sleeping bag into whirlpools around her feet. Megan, peering through the heads of grasses going yellow and dry, going to seed and feather. Megan excited by my tree.

"It's after something," she whispered.

A tree after something? After seed, in soil, and rain, of course. So why was Megan covering her mouth? Rapt by black branches, clustered foliage?

I screamed. At the dark swoop of leaves that plunged out of the tree and into the grass. At the squeak and screech of some small thing, lifted into a flapping sky. I'd never seen a bird of prey hunt outside of a television screen and I bounced, breathless, into a crouch beside Megan. The bird disappeared in the dark and we waited but the tree was steady, still, and after nothing after all.

At the veterinary surgery, our hospitalized birds eat frozen day-old chicks but this had been an owl, hunting in the grass, with eyes so much better than ours that he could see mice when we could barely see him.

I marvelled, "He must have been watching us all this time."

"What?"

Middle-earth to Megan. "This whole time, he could see us."

We looked up at the sky that was empty again and Megan said she'd never heard of hawks hunting at night. I said, "me neither." I felt like I should know the difference between a hawk and an owl, but it had moved so quickly, up and away.

I grew up on TV. Breakfast and after school. Mice fly in superhero suits. Animals talk and wear clothes. Cats and dogs chase each other, laugh, cry, and rescue injured and trapped children. Zorro's horse was cool, but as a child I was afraid of both Toronado and the blue plastic horse with red eyes you could ride for a quarter outside of Safeway.

"A small animal vet," I told my mom, who did not agree that my birthday gerbil would make a good visiting pet for her hospital's children's ward. I wanted to be a doctor like her, but I wanted to fix cats and dogs and gerbils. I dreamt about them, lined up in their beds, waiting for me to come by on rounds with a special stethoscope for hearing through fur. I'd bring them treats to eat if they felt well enough. If I had a kid she could pass the treats out, the way I did on weekends when my mom had to work. There wasn't much else for me to do but follow the candy stripers around with their cart of comics and mints. And later, steal the same for Andrew, who came to get his growth assessments done.

Three years deep in vet med my supervisor told me I needed to pick a project that we stood at least half a chance of getting funding for. When I shook Megan's hand the first time, my own had just come out of a cow's rumen. It had been gloved and was clean but was still incredibly warm. Megan was modelling the trajectory of methylmercury through northern ecosystems. I reached into the warm, wet bodies of cows to sample partially digested thistles and thorns.

Frames

Elbow deep in a live, second-hand, fistulated cow, a city kid wonders what they're doing in vet med. Neck deep in a moonlit field with a horrible conversationalist, I worried that Megan would wonder why she'd bothered coming. Then her hawk came down and caught us both up in watching for it to come back.

We brought binoculars the next time we had a free night but the moon wasn't out. The only things we could really see were distant headlights passing on the highway, and stars. Holes to heaven. Balls of gas. Points of light spreading apart and apart in the night. Tons of them, brighter without the moon.

"I did go back to the beach, Megan." The same beach on the edge of Nanaimo but this time I went down there because Andrew told me to fuck off so I did, storming down an asphalt path to the sudden dark of the unlit ocean. He wasn't a dwarf, he'd shouted at me. He had normal proportions, but none of the proteins that accept growth hormones, so there wasn't a ton his doctor (my mom) could do to make him grow. I'd told him I thought the official definition of dwarfism was four feet, ten inches and under.

We were eighteen, so I was done growing but he was still supposed to be. Incrementally. He'd lost all hope of passing my ribcage. I was not allowed to call him little. My bitter four-foot-eight friend. He asked me out to visit after his dad brought home brochures about bone-lengthening surgery. You could add a few inches, Andy, he'd said. You could reach the light switch, the paper towel in public bathrooms.

He is small, but Andrew manages fine with both light switches and paper towel dispensers. He's not that short. I recently watched him, drunk and rowdy, jump-start a motion-activated hand dryer beside a propped open men's room door. He danced under it, hands up, air ruffling his hobbit hair.

What I wanted to tell Megan was that, when I stormed away from Andrew, down to the beach, I was imagining a quiet splash and a row of ripples where the scooped side of a perfect pebble touched down on the water. I wanted a stone skipped perfectly, igniting circles of light. A redemptive chain of glowing.

I had looked it up by then. This phenomenon. Bioluminescence. But I've never had an arm for skipping stones. I made three feeble low-angle attempts before switching to monkey farts. For those you only have to throw a rock high enough up that it can fall straight down. A perfect ten diving stone hits the water without a splash or ripple and makes only a tiny, hiccupped sound. My monkeys farted in dark water that stayed dark.

I pushed a piece of driftwood into the water with my foot and it rolled away, wet and black in its shadow. I guessed maybe the water was too cold for the phosphorescent algae and ground the beach beneath the heel of my sneaker. There is light that comes from chemical reactions inside certain species of microscopic marine plankton that don't, apparently, grow in February off the coast of Nanaimo. Bioluminescence was very cool, but knowing that Andrew hadn't made anything happen two years ago left him less tricky, less magic than before.

I looked UFOs up too. I learned about freak cloud formations that are perfectly natural but don't form often enough for most people to know what they are. I researched hawks and found out that lots of them hunt at night, or at least in twilight. That it is at night that they are in greatest danger of swooping down in front of semis on the highway and having their wings caught in metal grilles. We had a few of those birds brought into the surgery. Most vet students perform their first euthanasia on injured wildlife. I looked into the blind eyes of a sixteen-year-old basset hound. "How about a movie, Megan, next time?" I asked.

"You said these weren't dates."

"No. No, but it's starting to look like UFOs might not exist."

Megan said of course they exist, we haven't identified every object that flies. But just because an object is unidentifiable by a couple of amateur sky watchers doesn't mean it's manned by aliens.

"Ladied by aliens?" I tried.

I don't think I meant them to be dates, per se. Our first trip, at least, really was about convincing Megan that she wouldn't see things if she didn't look for them. But our spot at the edge of the field got marked out by a rectangular patch of flattened grass. It never quite had time to recover from my need to watch and listen. From Megan's wanting to see another bird swoop down.

Our rectangle was at the end of a road that we only drove at night. It passed a fence that closed in what used to be a landfill. It was just a dark space inside a fence and I had never given much thought to it. We parked ten or twenty metres away from the end of the fence and walked out into the field and sipped from our thermos and ate our cheese, listening for sounds of the world that is awake when people are asleep. I listened to the difference between the wet, black ocean and our landlocked, life full, field.

I met Megan in biochemistry class but she didn't meet me. I blend into walls and I sit in back rows. I learned her name because she asked questions, all the time, every class. I thought she was beautiful. We didn't actually meet until Andrew came. He showed up at the veterinary emergency doors, exploding with big and secret news, and announced that he was taking over my couch for a couple of weeks. To visit. To calm down. To avoid his dad who did not quite approve of the job he was so excited about.

A week later, I was just pulling my arm out of Mrs. A7859's cannulated fistula when Andy popped into the barn lab with Megan trailing curiously behind him. The beautiful girl from biochem who I hadn't worked myself up to talking to yet, but had pointed out to Andrew in the quad. He's right charming when he wants to be, and hard to ignore. He'd invited her along to the pub session that Andrew and I were apparently meeting up for. She said, "I have two black belts," when we offered to walk her home.

Oh lanky poet veterinarian, Andy called me. Friend to all cats but afraid of cows. It was true. I had to make my cows eat thistles when their neighbours were munching oats. Then I reached into their stomachs to dig them back out. My cows were big and black as horses, with heavy stomping feet, and giant wet eyeballs that followed me donning my long green gloves. I waited all summer for one of them to snap and kick me.

I should never have told Andrew. But I did, and something also about their readily infected udder systems. I had said something about being off breasts.

"Hey Steph, got milk?" he greeted me, Megan at his shoulder.

"Thistles," I offered, blushing, and pointed to a Ziploc of puke green fibre and bile, just what I wanted to be associated with.

She was brave.

She poked the bag and petted the cow, and soon we were hanging out. Megan always laughing, Andrew more and more worked up about his secret job. Me awkward, excited, afraid and not afraid of Megan looking for whoever it was Andy seemed to be making me out to be. She really did have two black belts. One in karate, one in kung fu. And she was funny on top of smart. The week after Andy left, I got stuck for something to say and asked if she'd ever seen a UFO.

You can't see a tree for the lack of a forest sometimes. Miss things that are where you don't expect them to be, sort of a thing. We didn't see eleven deer all summer, Megan and me. They were right there, behind the landfill fence that we drove past again and again on the way to our field.

Frames

Twenty-eight orphans had been turned in to the university that summer. Eleven past the capacity of the petting farm and the stables of a parasite study combined. Veterinary Sciences ranched them out at the retired landfill, trusting the fence that kept the fossilizing baby diapers in to keep any predators out. There was forage and they trucked out water and extra feed. No one worried about the slightly rusted gate latch, mounted level with a four-month-old fawn's head. Level with the beginning antlers of a gangly white-tailed deer.

The man on the phone talked about blood over the crown of its head, in its eyes. He imagined juvies with slingshots, knives, or pellet guns. I dropped a half-digested thistle into the palm of a summer student, paged my supervisor, and rushed out to the truck with a medi-kit, lasso, PVC for splinting, and ever-handy duct tape. Dr. Ed brought a gun, tranquilizer cartridges, and bullets. In case, he said. But the buck was a tiny, trembling thing with stick-skinny legs. Tendons taut behind its knees. And half the 'blood' on its head turned out to be rust from the gate latch.

I caught him in a headlock. Held his bony shoulder against my ribs while he flapped his Bambi ears, stiff as rubber, against my neck. The deer was stronger than I'd expected, smaller but jumpier than my cows, and I had to pin him against the fence to keep him still while Dr. Ed cleaned his head, gave him an injection of antibiotics and another for tetanus. He left the gun lying in the grass near the gate. Metal shining black as the little guy's nose. Black as his eyes, focused ahead on his friends, backed away into the far corner of the lot. They were tall, outgrowing their speckled baby coats and almost ready to be shipped out to a preserve away from the city. I whispered that to the fawn, "three weeks left," before we let him go.

We capped the gate latch with PVC, so he couldn't worry his head anymore. Then we turned to watch him join the other deer.

They approached him, then sprang back, from the smell of the antiseptic, from the smell of my armpit lingering on his neck.

"They're bigger than I expected," Megan said, when I shone the flashlight through the fence. They'd never had to worry about food or running away from anyone but me and Dr. Ed.

"They are bigger than wild fawns, my deerling," I said.

But Megan was making cat noises, beckoning the fawns. They pressed soft mouths up to the fence to take grass from her hands. They scattered when I started the car, but gathered again to watch us drive away. Twenty-two eyes reflected our headlights, coupled coins in a linked metal net.

Megan by movie-light frowned seriously at the short that told us to turn off our cell phones. Our seats were joined and she frowned at me shifting forwards and back again. She reached her tongue out, deer-style, and pulled it into her mouth with popcorn clinging to the tip.

I shook my head, I couldn't eat.

"Relax," she whispered, "it's a long movie."

It was a long movie, and for most of it, they used computer animation to shrink normal-heighted actors into hobbits, but they hired real stunt doubles for the action scenes. Real stunt doubles to fight the Orcs with the Ents.

"S'Andrew!" I shouted, pointing. The people around us stared.

It was Andrew. From the front, just some actor acting. But from behind, Andrew jumping out of the arms of an Ent and landing in an awesome shoulder roll. It was Andrew. Lifted out of our lives. We poked each other, again and again, grinning in the dark, whispering, "It's Andy."

He's the one who imagined us first, Megan and me. Our hands brushing together in the popcorn, our fingers touching and rustling seeds.

Marrow

THERE'S NO BASEMENT IN MY GRANDMA'S house, just a place to turn around at the bottom of the stairs. My grandpa was going make a basement under the living room but he died first. Because he was drunk. Aunty Judy found him on her way to school in the morning but she didn't know it was Grandpa at first because the snow turned him into a lump in the middle of the path in the backyard. A long white lump. I knew it was his ghost at the bottom of the stairs because it felt so sad down there. Quiet and sad and all painted white. I knew there was a ghost because it felt so lonely.

After the first time I went down there with my mom, we told Grandma she should put her vegetables down there to keep them from going bad the way they do in the kitchen. It is so cold they wouldn't be able to rot. She frowned at first and then she told me you couldn't fit three bricks lengthwise down there. That is not true, though. There's room for three people to stand down there. There's room for three people to stretch. There's lots of room for vegetables but Grandma keeps her carrots and onions upstairs in a cupboard next to the fridge.

The warm air coming out of the fridge makes them go rotten and it spreads the smell all the way down to where the stairs get cold from the underground air. Grandpa's ghost could smell it there, vegetables and dinner cooking. Ghosts don't mind rotten things. I thought, he must get very, very hungry.

When Grandma's cat started pawing at the door to the stairs every time it was closed she said she would have to find her mousetrap from Canadian Tire.

But then the cat came upstairs with a piece of dried out salami and Grandma figured out that she doesn't have mice, she has a seven-year-old granddaughter. That is what she told Beatrice, her friend, on the phone. That is what she told Mom. At suppertime she told me that if I don't like the food I should say, "No thank you," and not waste it by throwing it away. She makes meat loaves shaped like cupcakes, but they still taste like meat loaves. Ketchup is not icing. I said, "No thank you."

"Eat." Mom said. Then she said, "Why do you want to go down there, anyway? It's creepy."

But it's not creepy. It is just very quiet. It's a space that needs company, which is the same thing as a ghost. I know Daddy told my mom that when she asked how could there be ghosts and reincarnation at the same time. The bottom of the stairs needed me for company. And if I was the only one who knew Grandpa was sitting down there, I had to be the one to get him exercised.

I didn't mind visiting, after I got used to it. It was fun, and dirty because of the floor being made out of dirt. Grandma always stayed in the kitchen so I could be down there all by myself, stretching and rolling around and walking on the stairs with my knees. Also practising headstands leaning on the wall with the door in it. That's the strangest thing about the bottom of the stairs. There's three walls and one of them has a door in it. There's nothing but dirt on the other side, Grandma said. The house moved after the door got put there so it doesn't open anymore. It's not locked but no one is ever going to be strong enough to open that door ever again. It's like the sword that won't come out of the rock unless King Arthur comes back from the dead. I pulled on the door handle but am not magic at all.

Marrow

I found the books Grandpa wrote when Grandma told me to lurk upstairs instead. They were in boxes under the dresses hung up in her closet. At first I thought Grandpa wrote a lot of books, but I showed my mom and she said they're all copies of the same one. A whole boxful of copies with black and gold covers, brand new. I thought maybe we could sell them, on the front lawn, like a book garage sale.

Mom said no.

I thought we could use the money for Grandma, to buy her something nice for letting us stay at her house for so long. Or we could hide it and make a treasure map to help her find it, for a surprise. But Mom said no, and she said we wouldn't make very much money anyway because the books are full of terrible poems. Poems too sad for people to read. She said the poems are mostly about things young men wish for, and that married men with one eye need to forget about.

That was the first time I found out that Grandpa only had one eye. In Grandma's pictures he has two, but one of them got lost in the war. He died a long time ago, before there were pirates, maybe, so he never wore an eye patch. Mom said his face looked crumpled but okay to look at, but Grandma never took a picture of him after he came back. It seemed like that might be a remorseful thing for a ghost, especially if he was sad already.

On Saturday, when my cousins Ryan and Tim came over, we were supposed to be running around on the grass so my mom and their mom and Grandma could talk in peace. Tim wanted to know why I was sad instead of being fun to play with. He thought I was mad because when they first came over Ryan wanted to go into Grandma's raspberries, which prickle and have spiders. Spiders are poisonous, sometimes, but it wasn't that really. Tim wanted to know why I was being quiet so I told him about Grandpa being stuck one-eyed at the bottom of the stairs. Then Tim said we had to tell Ryan because he's their grandpa too. So I told Ryan about how Grandpa needed company and how usually I gave him exercise in the afternoon.

"What kind of exercise?" Ryan wanted to know. "All kinds," I said, in the dark. But when Mom found all three of us exercising down there she made Grandma find a lamp.

It wasn't as spooky or sad down there all lit up. It was still fun to exercise, though, and upstairs in the kitchen we could hear Aunt Judy laughing and moving chairs and telling my Mom "Oh, let them be, kids are kids." They were just glad I think how we were all getting along.

I showed Ryan and Tim how to do headstands. You have to tip over and then you can jump and kick your feet, like swimming up, upside down. Tim could do it. And Ryan tried. Except Ryan is a lot bigger than Tim and me and when he did his headstand he kicked his foot all the way through the door that doesn't open.

That door is painted white but at the broken part we could see how it is really made out of wood. I felt like Grandpa might get mad that we broke the door that he must have had a hard time making out of wood with only one eye and his old-fashioned tools. Grandpa's tools are still in Grandma's garage and they are really old. They stay under a tarp made out of stinky fabric — not like the blue plastic tarp that Tim and Ryan's dad keeps on top of the boat that fills up his whole driveway. Their dad has that boat but he never took them on it yet, but Ryan said he's going to next time they go. I was going to say, big deal, because my daddy probably could have a boat if he wanted one. But then Tim said, "Hey you guys, maybe we should tell Brian and he would be able to fix the door." Brian is Aunty Judy's new boyfriend. He's not really their dad.

"No," I said, "we should tell our moms."

Marrow

But Ryan is the one whose foot did it and he said, "You guys, listen, this is a secret."

We went upstairs very quietly and unplugged the lamp and then we closed the door at the top of the stairs and went to Grandma's room and watched the movie that Tim and Ryan's actual dad gave Ryan for his birthday. That movie was kind of funny but I kept feeling Grandpa being sad and disappointed underneath us. He was wondering why I bothered exercising him if I was just going to wreck everything and make his door into a secret. Ryan said he knew a better way to exercise ghosts that we could do next time to make Grandpa go away so he couldn't be mad at me leaving him alone anymore. I wanted Ryan to tell me but he said, "You have to wait, Chaya. This is going to be a secret too."

I dreamed that Grandpa came upstairs and dripped water out of his missing eyehole onto my bed until it started floating. When my mom came she said I peed the bed but I didn't. I tried to explain that I just couldn't get Grandpa to stop crying on me. In my dream, he said, "You're made up more of marrow than bones." Like that meant I was a sponge to suck up how sad he was.

My mom rubbed her face, and then she asked if I miss my dad sometimes.

My daddy used to say things about what we're made out of to make my mom roll her eyes. Like crystals vibrating. Also energy balls.

"I miss my dad too," Mom said.

She was kneeling down close to me, holding on to my arms so she wouldn't get wet. She tried to look at me but I know she doesn't really miss my dad very much. She gets a lot more sleep now.

After lunch, Grandma came looking for me to go for tea at Beatrice's and she saw the hole in the door because I went halfway down the stairs to look at it. I wanted to know if Grandpa was still there.

Grandma looked at the hole in the door and said, "Chaya, is this your doing?"

I was on the stairs and she was in the doorway holding up the lamp. I wanted to say it wasn't me but I didn't want to say it was Ryan's foot because she's his grandma too. Grandma put the lamp down and actually came downstairs and went around me to pick up a sliver off the dirt at the bottom of the stairs. She held it up for me to look at and she said, "Honestly."

She wanted me to say what happened, but I could see that the lamp wasn't shining off anything on the other side of the hole in the door. It was showing me a black space. A cave on the other side. A cave with dripping water and stalagmites, I thought. A ghost or a pirate cave. I was quiet for so long that Grandma thought I was sorry.

She said, "It's just an old door."

She said that at Beatrice's house too, and "She misses her daddy."

We left him in Toronto so we could come home.

Grandma and Beatrice were knitting donkeys for Afghanistan. I had to sit at Beatrice's table with them and wind red wool in and out around a fork to make flowers for the donkey baskets. They looked more like fireworks than proper flowers. Also, I saw Afghanistan before on the news and it is a place that has blizzards and a war. If I lived in a war and instead of food or band-aids I got a stuffed knitted donkey with baskets full of my flowers stuck on the sides of it, I don't think I would like it.

"Maybe we should make some socks," I said.

"Oh my," Beatrice said, "doesn't she sound like her father."

Grandma raised up her eyebrows.

"Chaya," Beatrice said, "you must just break your mother's heart."

I don't do that.

Grandma snorted. "Chaya, God means for children to play, no matter where they live."

I don't break my mom's heart. And about what Grandma said, if it's true then she shouldn't be allowed to make me sit in Beatrice's kitchen winding wool around her forks.

It was Tim's idea that he should bring over his flashlight when they came for supper so we could look inside the hole properly and it was Ryan's idea that we should read Grandpa's poems backwards to exercise him away.

"Backwards every word or just words in backwards order?" I wanted to know.

Ryan said we should put Xs of water on our foreheads first and unplug the lamp. I was scared we would see bats or cave rats in the dark, maybe. Tim said maybe he didn't want to look if there were rats in there and that, no, he wouldn't unplug the lamp because his hands had water on them and he wasn't stupid.

"Fine," Ryan said, "Chaya, you do it."

I had water on my hands too, though, from making the X that was dripping onto my nose. Ryan said we were babies and pulled the cord out himself. Then it was very dark because we had closed the door at the top of the stairs so Ryan had to turn on Tim's flashlight before he started reading "waiting lamplight the in ladies . . ." which made me embarrassed, because of bathrooms, ladies and gentleman's. Embarrassed and scared because then Ryan turned the flashlight up to shine on the door and it made the hole look like a skinny mouth with pieces of broken white door for teeth. It looked like a monster crying. Tim said he definitely didn't want to look in there anymore, but Ryan said he had to, and then suddenly I felt mad because why would Grandpa care if Tim looked in there or not? There was just dirt there anyway, not monsters or pirates. Grandma said so.

Ryan read "out held hands and hearts pass bus . . ." and I said "Stop!" because what if we did make Grandpa go away? He was sad and lonely but I didn't really want him to go away. I wanted him to be happy, not to go away. Ryan said, "Chaya, shut up," but I said, "no." Then Ryan said, "Chaya, shut up," again and Tim said I wouldn't shut up, I'd throw up and he'd make Ryan lick it up. Then Ryan said, "Tim, shut up! Chaya, look at the door," because I was going to go upstairs, and Tim said "You can't make her do anything!" and then it got bright suddenly because Mom and Aunty Judy opened the kitchen door and both of them shouted "Honestly!"

My mom lifted me and Tim up so we could point the flashlight in through the hole and see a tiny closet with a shelf on it.

We could read a sign on a box on the shelf that said 'ONIONS'.

"It's the cold storage room, that's all," she said. "The house moved and the door doesn't open anymore, that's all."

But Ryan got in trouble upstairs, with Aunty Judy yelling at him, and then she told Brian to get the boys in the car because the visit was over. Grandma said we all of us should know better but she rubbed her hand up and down on my back.

The next day me and Grandma and Mom made soup out of leftovers and the vegetables that had got too close to the borderline. Dirt-smelling vegetable and meatloaf soup. In the box with the wrinkly potatoes there was one that was really shrivelled up with new leaves coming out of its top. I showed my mom and she said, "Neato mosquito!"

Mom cut the green top off with a hunk of potato. Then we took the spidery eyes grandma was cutting off of the other potatoes away from her cat, who likes to chew on them. And we got some of the bendy carrots out of the compost bucket and cut the tops off of them too. We put all those vegetable bits together in a saucer and added some water and put the saucer on the windowsill where they'd get sunshine.

"This is real magic," my mom said, "the kind we wait and see for."

The potato leaf got bigger and the veggie bits grew little see-through roots after three days, but then Grandma's cat drank all the water out of the saucer and all of those vegetables dried up and died. Mom said that if it wasn't for the cat they would have made whole new plants. "In time," she said. Maybe in about two weeks, I think. Next time we're going to put the saucer on top of the fridge, away from the cat, and when the new plants grow big enough I'm going to move them into dirt outside. We could grow a whole garden full of vegetables that way. But Grandma's not going to fix the door at the bottom of the stairs so it can open. She let Brian nail a new piece of wood over the hole in the door but she's not going to bother letting him fix it to open like he says he could even though she could keep all her vegetables and everything from my garden from going bad down there.

She said it would be a big job and the stairs are too steep for her old legs anyway but it's not true because the stairs going up to her bedroom are just as steep and she goes up and down them all the time.

Tim said maybe Grandma likes to keep her potatoes warm so they'll grow those spidery eyes for her cat to play with. Or maybe Grandma likes having to eat carrots really fast so that one day she might eat enough to be able to see in the dark for a little while.

Aunty Judy said that that wouldn't really happen, that it's just a story to make kids eat carrots. But I don't know. I think most kids like carrots anyway.

Ryan said maybe Grandma likes having her kitchen smell like vegetables to help her remember how Grandpa loved her so much that he dug a whole room underground for her with his bare hands. It's smaller than a room, though, you know. It's more like a closet. And I'm sure he used a shovel.

Carys

SHE WONDERED WHY HE HAD DESCRIBED it as a housefly. A lentil or coffee bean is the same size. A ladybug. There are nicer objects in that size class. But the doctor had said not much bigger than a housefly and she could see one now. Appearing to hover, wasp-like, near the lamp sconce above the porch where a movement of air twisted the web that the fly had been caught in. Its body trailed at the end of a broken strand.

The beauty of math, Michelle reflected, is that it can prove. A theorem can exist with an interior wholeness, a prism of logic. Whereas science tests and trials; medicine works in the dark. He had assured them that their embryo was developing normally. But it was obvious to Michelle now, as indeed it had been even then, that anything capable of coming to life is also capable of dying. That women of child-bearing age are equally capable of hosting death.

The improbable housefly with its detectable heartbeat had been Matthew and Michelle's fifth and last conception. Michelle suspected the universe of knowing that she had stopped hoping properly. The irony was the previous twenty years of birth control. When the housefly was pointed out on the screen, ten weeks along, Michelle had been unable to believe that its blinking heartbeat would relieve them of spoiling other people's children. She doesn't think Matthew has realized even now that she mailed the retainer to the breeder before the miscarriage. Three days before it. So that two months later Vernon would arrive, a distractingly loveable mess of a puppy.

Michelle hid the bears that Matthew propped enthusiastically in the spare room after the first three appearances of double pink lines on home pregnancy tests. Two years after the last miscarriage she wrapped the white bear as a hasty gift for the child of a cousin who dropped by unexpectedly the day before Christmas. The black bear went with flowers to an older friend, hospitalized by a stroke. The brown bear, bought during one of the middle pregnancies whose details she doesn't wholly remember, remains in their closet behind a stack of sweaters. If the housefly had grown, that bear would have been hers. Michelle knows that it would have been a girl — a poor sleeper, who would wake her mother throughout the night well into childhood.

Recently, the only way to get the child to sleep has been to bring her into their bed where the wheeze of Matthew's snoring can lull her to sleep. Michelle falls asleep listening to her daughter's breath, soft beneath Matthew's, disrupted only by Vernon who scrabbles and whimpers through hunting dreams at the foot of their bed. At night, she has no issue with a daughter who can both exist and not exist. If pressed to explain, she might attempt a proof circling uncertainty, and the difficulty of proving one's own existence, much less another being's. She has held the housefly through her sleep for six years. More interesting than proof are the potentials of probability. Quantum theory and math agree, after all, that we live in a multiverse.

On the porch, beneath the dead husk of the hovering fly, and beside a kinder view of red geraniums and lawn, Michelle has been reviewing the details of two courses that she will begin teaching in three days. The fly has strained her focus. Reminding her of their stalled child and the fact that death, not birth, has made a mother of her. Michelle has the seniority to pawn off her undergraduate classes, but secretly enjoys meetings with weepy students after exams. And openly enjoys the enthusiastic ones, coming in with questions, new ideas, articles to show her. She recognizes their nervous rawness, a quality she had herself once, and enjoys the shock each fall as her students grow younger. All science majors are now required at least a passing familiarity with statistics, which to Michelle entails an ability to discern the value of their thoughts and the magnitude of their problems. She has never seriously considered backing away from her teaching, regardless of the department's drive for research publications. Neither has Matthew. They are at their best neck deep in busyness and are at loose ends when it is punctuated by holidays. Michelle's last-minute course revisions have been brought about by a quick, unplanned trip to an August conference in the UK. She came home to find their dining-room table, desks, and floors covered with Matthew's lesson plans. Now he is tidying, clearing space for her resettlement while she works on the front porch. Expanding in Michelle's absence is Matthew's guilty pleasure. This and sharing people food with Vernon, who appreciates Matthew's cooking with an enthusiasm rarely equalled by humans.

At her conference in the UK, around the world from Matthew, Michelle missed the cup of coffee-syrup he usually handed her for breakfast. By noon she was hungry enough to face the conference buffet table, strewn with used styrofoam cups, stir sticks, and crumpled muffin cups that had recently held crustless sandwiches. Michelle was swallowing her second of the sandwiches, devilled egg, and battling a headache that weak British coffee wasn't helping with when she saw the girl. She was standing by one of the poster-board displays lining the hallway. A group of men in belly-strained dress shirts obscured the girl's research so Michelle was forced to look at the girl herself. Her hair was pulled back in a tidy ponytail with a sparkly barrette holding her bangs back from her forehead. Michelle imagined lip-gloss, bubblegum flavoured, in her pocket. The girl had dressed for a junior high school band concert in a black skirt and crisp white blouse. The graduate students, too, were getting achingly young.

With a program abstract containing one small grammatical error, Michelle was stepping in for a colleague to present a co-authored paper coupling glacial retreat to the advance of groundwater parasites. It was an interesting and novel model — a pasting of mathematical abstraction to the realities of ice and environmental biology. Applications were key to both progress and funding. Pure mathematics were problematic — they enticed with certainty, but slid so easily into ambiguity unless modelled and tethered down.

Matthew worked in applied geometry, which had ready applications to structural architecture, and he attracted graduate students destined to design and engineer. Michelle had trained three mathematical historians, but she moved easily herself between the purities of proofs and probability to Matthew's realm of geometrical resonance. In his world 'honeybee' meant slightly larger than a housefly, and it meant a hexagonalist; a subscriber to the pattern adopted by drying mud, growing quartz, and cooling basaltic magma. Matthew was a pattern-seeker. Their own pattern was so obvious that when they reflected back together, they did so with a sense of almost pride. If fifteen percent miscarry between six and twelve weeks, and seventy-six percent go on to have a live birth after one miscarriage, and seventy percent go on to a live birth after two or three deaths, and even sixty percent have a baby after four miscarriages — Matthew and Michelle were statistical rarities. All the more special because no test had ever identified a problem with either one of them. They ducked both odds and explanations.

The second day of the conference, the girl wore a blue skirt and a pale green, somewhat school-girlish blouse with oxford loafers to present a paper on the linguistics of math education, which was more than overshadowed by new work on the Rare Earth Equation. The Rare Earth theory posits that the type and age of star, of planet, and of chemistry necessary to support life are incredibly uncommon in the universe. And that a string of highly unlikely and random events are required to draw an accidental arrangement of organic molecules towards the evolution of functioning microbialism. The presentation negotiated the exact improbability of human life, to Michelle's impatience. The difficulty of proving our existence aside, our existence is a caveat to considering the likeliness of our existence. Obvious, but the conference room was filled to standing space.

The girl, slotted randomly to precede the feature lecture, presented a simple survey proving that the languages of math learning, math literacy, and primary linguistic fluency are strongly interdependent. Hence, migrant employees had a preset performance disadvantage in Britain's technological workspaces. There were no questions. The girl blushed herself aside as the Rare Earthers swept in. And Michelle found herself angry with the girl's supervisor. For allowing that presentation slot. For the slim connection of the girl's work to the conference theme of Math and Sustainability. The paper was in fact strong, but out of place. She supposed that it suited the supervisor's agenda to bring the girl along, rather than find a more fitting venue for her work. Michelle was careful with her own students, bringing them first to present at small, nurturing conferences. Where experts could be easily approached. Where emeriti would be likely to step in with thoughtful commentary and advice. And she would have counseled the girl to wear slacks. She had erred into the crisp and anonymous fashion sense of waitresses and flight hostesses. Attempts at impression can easily be mistaken for insubstantiality in a discipline dominated by men.

Matthew and Michelle had discussed adoption. After years of browbeating conception, the discussion was abrupt.

"Do you want to adopt, we'd be good candidates I think . . ."

"No," Michelle had replied. "We've been over this before."

Although, somehow, they actually hadn't. They hadn't discussed it at all, though each had given the idea individual attention. In this attempted conversation they lay in bed, he with his arms crossed behind his head in a stiff effort to look relaxed, she with hers crossed over the duvet, pulling it tight against her chest. Matthew suggested going out for breakfast. Michelle agreed, but couldn't explain why she didn't want another person's baby. Except that she felt smotheringly nervous at the idea of assuming that responsibility when she had so easily, and repeatedly, misplaced her own babies. She suspects, to a depth that Matthew does not, that they have been rerouted from parenthood by something more or less purposeful. She does not believe in God, and this is only partly because of issues surrounding his/her provability. She can feel the child beside her when she relaxes, but nothing larger than that.

The conference delegates were housed in student residences, vacant over the summer. So it was in a shared washroom that Michelle woke suddenly at five a.m. to be violently ill. She shared the washroom with a Dr. Simi Sidhu from Indonesia, a woman she had encountered at other international conferences but with whom she was only passingly friendly. Wiping a spot of bile from the toilet seat and hoping Simi was a solid sleeper, Michelle puzzled over the remains of the prior evening's meal before flushing. Her first thought was food poisoning, but the nausea didn't last or return. Jet lag was also a stomach stressor for her sometimes. Maybe she'd swallowed a fly — it wriggled and jiggled and squiggled inside her.

If the girl's name hadn't been Carys, quite close to the Kerry they'd had on their list, or if she hadn't dressed up, in sequined shoes, for the conference 'banquet', Michelle might not have fully suspected that she was pregnant. It was hard to believe, but equally impossible to ignore with the girl seated only three tables away. A math conference banquet is not a real banquet and is definitely not something that you dress up for. Most of the attendees were in the crumpled shirts and slacks they'd lounged around the conference in all day, corded name tags either dangling into their meals or tucked above neck ties that swayed, left and right, not unlike Vernon's drool strings after a long run at the dog park. But the girl had taken the invitation to a banquet at face value and wore a soft brown dress and sequined, gold ballet flats. Mistakes Michelle would never have made because even in their youth Matthew had screened her outfits at the door.

When the meal and keynote lecture faded to drinks and debating on the lawn outside the faculty club's French doors, Michelle saw that the girl had kicked her shoes off. Carys was chatting with two other students, swinging her jewelled slippers by their heels beneath a crossed arm, her toes bare in the grass, while Michelle's were hugged in knee-high nylons and walking shoes. Her daughter was relaxed, laughing out of place because the event didn't matter. Not in the wider sense of her life opening, branching, and growing.

Alone that night in the twin student residence bed, Michelle found herself missing the housefly's breath. She missed the curve of bundled sheets that built the imagined body, nestled between its parents. That child had appeared and set up residence in Michelle's life as easily as Vernon had in Matthew's. But now there was new nausea, along with mild but ambitious bloating. And this girl, Carys Anderson, who by her awkwardness in the conference rooms and her ease on the lawn, had made herself endearing and familiar. It was incredibly easy to imagine being the girl's supervisor. To imagine the better job Michelle could do of it. And it would have ended there if Michelle's breasts hadn't ached and swelled so determinedly through dinner. If a little creature was burrowing into her, Michelle felt no need to reach for a test. Not when the beginnings of life were as familiar to her as the end of it.

The Drake Equation preceded the Rare Earth hypothesis. Back in the sixties, Frank Drake estimated the number of civilizations likely to be present inside our Milky Way galaxy. He considered rates of star formation, the number of planets around existing stars, the likelihood that those planets would be capable of, and that some actually would, support life, and the overarching probability that all these factors would come together at the same time inside infinity. In his model, the probability of life existing ex-terra was quite high. It would be a typical product of rocky planets positioned 'just so' from their stars. The fact that we have yet to meet another civilization formed the guts of Fermi's Paradox. With a twist, the universe appeared to favour the least probable reality. But in the wilds of time, most things are improbable, at least briefly. This paradox grounds the universe. Perhaps it is not the fact of a living Earth but the fact of its loneliness that is improbable.

Michelle called Matthew after the banquet, wakening him to share an insight gleaned from an overheard conversation and to hear a sleepy account of Vernon's recent antics. She had watched the girl getting into a taxi with a couple of other students, brushing off the older generation for a celebratory pub night. She had yearned momentarily for the energy that had sparked between her and Matthew in their student days. If it were possible, she would be pregnant now with that girl. A girl already born and approaching the wildest stage of alive. This was an enticing musing, and Michelle felt an unfamiliar optimism that she would be able to embrace the trials of creating life if the result were so certain. This girl had even followed her own unlikely path into math. Imagining her daughter, Michelle missed exactly what Vernon had done with a new chew toy, but laughed when Matthew did. She sent kisses over the wires to her husband and dog. And wondered if it is easier to love, too, in your most fluent language. Hers was the dialogue between questions likely and unlikely, possible or not. Most love is probably unintended.

Hedging bets, and feeling only slightly silly, Michelle drank a cup of decaf Earl Grey instead of coffee at breakfast. If she were pregnant, she wasn't going to jinx the process. She was hoping to introduce herself to her daughter that morning and had come up with an idea to discuss, one that might move the girl's project towards publication. This tangible connection might have dissipated the improbable fantasy. But when Michelle ventured over to the poster displays the girl wasn't there. Was off at a presentation, perhaps, or sleeping off her previous night. And maybe it was better for Michelle that the girl wasn't there. She looked so much like Matthew, after all, and had blushed like him too, at the end of her presentation the day before. She was shy about her work, the way Matthew had been once.

On the phone the night before, Michelle had resisted telling Matthew that her nipples felt heavy. Pinched, as though someone was attempting to tune her in, using them as radio dials. With no one physically present to confide in, it felt safer and easier to keep the news to herself. She attempted to escape from the conference to a library but found that it had been recently redone and reeked of fresh carpet, glue, and ammonia. The path leading around the side of the library emerged into a maze of shrubbery and a wide, open view of the sky. The idea of unsettling Matthew and Vernon with an infant's needs, of forcing a year's maternity leave into her upcoming sabbatical, felt large and unreal. But by the fourth and last day of the conference, Michelle found she was able to ask Matthew what he thought of the name.

The sessions were ending. Michelle had packed earlier in the day, and bending over her carry-on, had been brought to her knees by a sharp abdominal pain. As her Rare Earth colleagues stressed, it is the death of stars and the birth of black holes that typifies the universe. The sky is black not white because light dies and the space between stars is far greater than the size of the stars themselves. Death hurts but it is also a solid certainty. It can be sudden, but it is unmistakable. And the names they had picked out six years ago were passé, well used. Name trends interested Michelle. They ran mysteriously parallel between couples despite almost everyone attempting to hold their choices close. For years Michelle had kept their list on a spreadsheet and had crossed off eight of their favourite ten girl names as emails came announcing the births of nieces, second cousins, and friend's babies. She hadn't thought of baby names for awhile, but asking Matthew felt so right — "Do you like Carys?"

"Carys?"

"It means love in Welsh."

Michelle hadn't mentioned the girl. Not even a small funny detail like her sequined shoes. Not her hair and eyes the colour of Matthew's. Not her project that could be made more rigorous. So it pleased her when Matthew said, well, actually, he liked the name quite a lot. He couldn't know how taken Michelle was with the idea. Her relief, not to have to imagine another child into life. The incredible release hidden inside the disappointment of not having actually talked to the girl one-on-one — knowing so little, it was easier to let her go. And maybe there was no reason to be excited; this could be something else. Like the start of menopause, which should not be that far off.

"Did you want to get her from the same breeder?" Matthew asked.

He had been talking about a companion for Vernon for a few months. He worried that Vernon was getting bored when they were away for the day. Taken off guard by his question, Michelle forgot her own premonition that two bored dogs would be worse for the condition of their house than one. She tripped over the thread of his question, reached out and caught, "Of course."

They had lost the housefly at ten weeks when the mere fact of her heartbeat indicated a ninety percent chance at viability. Their child had bones in her arms, and in the ultrasound she had kicked and spun tumble turns around the axis of her cord. Watching a documentary, Michelle had learned that Tibetan toddlers are tethered to keep them safe — tied a bright scarf's radius short of knives and cooking fires. NASA's astronauts tie themselves to boards with Velcro straps at night because it gives their bodies the illusion of gravity and the familiarity of sleeping with a 'down.' Navajo babies traditionally slept in similar constraints, tied into stiff-backed papooses by parents aware that babies can float away at night.

On the return flight Michelle pressed her back into her seat and pictured a starry cluster of energy slipping down through the fibres of the carpet. A soul dissipating through the underlay. Going back to space and stars. A return from possibility to mystery. She longed to curl around the housefly's body. Dreaming about that child, dreaming with that child, had achieved the same deep familiarity as remembering. It was possible for Michelle to pretend that the ache in her back was from lifting and porting that child. From not protecting her posture or denying the child carrying once she had really grown to big for it. She had kept her housefly alive against all odds and had never really wanted to let that child go, not even to make space. So it was a relief not to have told Matthew anything. Only to have asked about the name.

Michelle opened the follow-up email from the conference organizers eagerly. It was a thank-you for participating. A 'what a raving success' review. A polite plea for timely submission of articles for the proceedings. And the obligatory group photos. Pictures that held Michelle, possibly, briefly pregnant. She found herself in the first photo, asexually dressed and sandwiched between two suited Asian postdocs in the second row. Her roommate Simi was in a pink suit on the left side of the group. Another acquaintance, Richard, was looking worse for wear at the far end of the third row. Michelle looked for but didn't see the girl. In the second attachment a couple of the British student volunteers had jumped in at the side of the front row but Carys wasn't there yet. She was in the third photo. Apparently present the whole time but only then exposed, as Richard turned his bulk to beckon to someone off camera. Carys had turned to see this person too. The girl's hand was raised over her face to catch her hair, loosed from its ponytail and swinging forwards. Next she would tuck her hair back, in behind her ear, and expose her face. Michelle had an urge to lean in to the computer, but Matthew was beside her in the kitchen, handing her coffee, and peering in himself. Michelle rested the cup's warmth against her lips. Imagined the smooth warmth of the girl's hair. Matthew picked her out and grimaced, "Not your best picture, babe, is it?"

Tell

I TOOK SO LONG OVER MY cup of tea and pita wrap that tables were already filling up for storytelling by the time I contemplated dessert (peanut pie or carrot crumble). I sat tight and ducked the cover charge. Carol's Café is a performance venue for the Ears to Hear Festival and the stage had a three storyteller, two folk musician line-up that night. I was trying to decide whether to stick around or not when a granola girl in brightly coloured, if shoddily crafted, woollies plopped into the seat beside me.

"Don't you work at the library?" She smiled and pulled her toque and scarf off with a conspiratorial squint.

Being a librarian lends a bit of celebrity, but mostly its kids who pipe up and point in grocery stores. I nodded and tried to look modest.

She told me that she always admires my French braids. She was grinning and it was a nice thing to say, but I find it hard to react appropriately to compliments from strangers. I often lie. I told her that my mother had been German and trained me in traditional hair braiding and ekrousak embroidery from the time I was a little girl.

She nodded abstractedly.

I was glad she didn't ask after the 'had been'. I hadn't decided if my mother was dead or had just disowned her nationality. Don't ask me what ekrousak embroidery might be.

"I just can't wait to see this guy," she said. "He's amaaaayzing."

I liked the way her woolly clothing smelled, and I wasn't ready to face the mess in my bathroom . . . I smiled and rubbed my hands in anticipation.

"What's with the bracelet?" she asked, eyes on a band of duct tape I'd wrapped around my wrist.

"Oh, you know . . ." I began. I was going to say something about archery, but the storyteller came out and crackled the mike.

He was amazing to look at. His name was Gustav Gorav and he had a striped beard that rested on his knees when he sat on the stool in front of the mike. His teeth were so large that I could pick out their individual borders from halfway across the café. He had bright red suspenders with crimps that bit into a thick green belt looped through his drooping jeans. Apparently, Gustav had no issues with redundancy. He pulsed his eyebrows up and down in a rhythm that had nothing to do with the cadence of his words.

Once upon a time in a land that is less of a place and more of an idea, the wind moved into a woman's womb and swirled in eighteen circles . . .

The story was interrupted by some microphone static and a high electric shriek. A teenager in a volunteer T-shirt bent over some cords and knobs. Gustav stroked his beard and began again:

Once upon a time the wind moved into a woman's womb and swirled in eighteen small circles. Circles that were the same size as two hands, two arms, two feet, two legs, two ears, two eyes, two nostrils, two lungs, one brain, and one beating heart. And as the circles spun, they separated from the wind, and they became lonely. Missing the safety of the wind's confederacy, they merged to form a small crescent. A crescent.

Gustav drew a 'C' in the air, nodded, and scratched his chin through his beard.

Tell

*A crescent that looked first like a fish, then like a chicken, and
then, when it had just begun to look like a monkey, the wind grabbed
its tail and pulled it out of the womb and into the world. Whoosh!*

Whoosh is one of those words that reminds me of dying, not
being born, but I kept listening, to be polite, waiting for my carrot
crumble. In children's acquisitions, we deal a lot in comics. Phoom!
Taka! Kapow!

*The monkey was surprised, but when he looked around, he
found that he quite liked the world. He liked the way that rain fell
and trees reached up to meet it. He liked the animals that circled
about, sniffing his head and tickling his ears with licking tongues.
He liked the mangoes that the wind carved out of cloud for him
to eat. But most of all he liked the people and their seriousness.
He liked seriousness the way that black likes white and day likes
night — it made him lighthearted. He liked the people and their
foolishness — it made him wise. And all of this lightheartedness
and wisdom made him confident so that he was afraid of neither
death nor life, and when sunlight caught the monkey's laughter in
its web one dewy morning . . . the wind anointed him with oil: a
monkey god.*

Gustav held his hand out to his audience, palm upwards, and
rocked it slightly side to side so that we imagined him cupping a
ball. When we saw its weight roll in his palm, he tossed it gently
towards his left shoulder and brought an index finger forward to
rest against the microphone.

*What you must remember is that a monkey brought to godhood
is a monkey still. Hanuman leaped on the wind, shrieked as he
swung from the stars and the rafters of the temples and, when the
moon disappeared in the clouds, he stole mangoes.*
Oh, how he stole mangoes!

More mangoes than there are ants in the earth and fish in the sea!

Gustav began to wave his hands, conjuring multitudes of fruit, but my focus was caught on the toothed crimp that held his left suspender to the green belt. How many strawberries grow in the sea? Yesterday was a really, really bad day. Coyote, Raven, Anansi, Monkey-god day. As many red herrings as grow in the wood.

It had rained while I was walking to work at the library and a blue Volkswagen Jetta sped through a puddle at the edge of the sidewalk and soaked me with muddy water. My pants didn't dry until noon, by which time the chill was permanent. It added to a pre-existing pall my ex-boyfriend had cast over the day. The evening before he decided to call to thank me for teaching him some 'really important life lessons' and to ask whether I'd mind him dating my ex-best friend. Did I mind? Was I going to forbid such a thing? How could I? I might have had some say in the matter back when they actually started dating, i.e. when he was supposed to be my boyfriend and she was supposed to be my friend. But really, what business of mine was it what they did with each other? I didn't own them, hadn't owned them, had no proprietary rights to the dispensation of their love. What did I care if two idiots wanted their consciences cleared?

The people, serious and foolish, and bereft of sustenance due to Hanuman's thievery, gnawed the wind and moaned. Daggers of emptiness scraped at the bowls of their bellies. Krishna stomped his smooth blue feet.

Hanuman, the wind cried, you are summoned to the pantheon.

I kind of wanted to try this with Colton and Nancy . . . to haul them up in front of a righteous and moralizing god who could curse them and whoever was growing in the pregnant belly she'd been trying to disguise with a bulky sweater when she came to find me at the library. I was fighting an urge to spit, and then she asked me to be her maid of honour. Said how much she'd always admired me and how she wanted me to be in their child's life. Also, she wanted to treat me to Belgian hot chocolate with whipped cream, another person trying to fatten me up. I tried to feel superior and angry but my co-worker June piped up that my coffee break was only five minutes off. Nancy loitered in among the board books, then led me by elbow to the Starbucks in the foyer.

I listened, nodded, and tried desperately to insert some other topics into the conversation, but she wanted approval. I choked on the whipped cream, bent, and did her a favour. I told Nancy I could probably convince my uncle to rent them the Legion Hall half price. I told her I thought I could get them a Saturday in June.

Monkey that he was, when Hanuman heard the summons of the God, he grabbed a handful of mangoes and hid with his conscience in a dark and quiet cave. He hid there until he had eaten all the fruit. Hanuman hid and the wind queried the stones about his whereabouts, and he bribed the stones to silence with soft monkey songs.

This time, I wasn't lying or stretching anything. My uncle Larry's in charge of Legion Hall rentals. My aunt Christine is a caterer. I'm a great one to get involved in a wedding. But I guess I knew that they weren't just after that. They actually seemed to have sprouted morals of a sort. They actually seemed to need me to say yes, I do. Will. So I did, brave and ever eloquent. Yes (whatever), Nancy, enjoy.

But no one can sing in the darkness forever — and monkeys like trees and fruit and sun and, most of all, wind. And the very second that Hanuman crawled into the sunlight, the Gods saw him and beckoned him again.

Now the famine was over because the monkey had not stolen a single mango since he had crawled into the cave. As a matter of fact, the world had missed him. People missed his wisdom next to their foolishness. They missed his laugh because it gave them cause for seriousness. The Gods missed him too and weren't inclined to be stern.

Hanuman, they asked, why did you take mangoes that weren't yours?

How do you know that they weren't my mangoes? the monkey asked back, I saw no labels on the fruits that I ate. How was I to know that the trees did not bear them for me?

The Jaguar tugged at his beard. Hanuman, if you thought that the mangoes were yours why did you crawl into a cave when we called you?

This confused the monkey. If the Gods had known his whereabouts, why didn't they find him? Why didn't Giridhara lift the mountain that hid his cave or the Mouse Woman crawl through the cracks that led into the cave?

Aha! Perhaps the Gods had not known his whereabouts. Perhaps they had only seen him when he crawled out of the cave and now pretended to have known where to find him all along.

Dear sirs and madams, Hanuman said, I was not in a cave though I did come through a cave as I returned from bestowing blessings in the temple.

Really? Laxmi asked, What temple was this?

Ah, lied Hanuman, it was the temple of the fifth pillar.

What now? I could lie to them but not to myself about being okay with things. After my coffee break, Nancy went to Pilates but I had to go back to work. Struggling through publishers' catalogues for children's books that could compete with TV, I was in every way obsolete. The emotions swirling through me — jealousy, anger, loss — had no right to exist.

How do I explain what happened next? Have you ever behaved the way that you felt you were expected to behave? Have you ever, in deep emotion, found yourself following a maze of clichés? Found yourself smiling at unfunny jokes because this is what one does with jokes? Found yourself hugging someone you dislike because they've opened their arms in front of you? Found yourself whispering 'I love you' to someone you don't love (may hate) because they've said the words to you? Have you ever found falsity easier than navigating half-understood truths?

Arriving home, still chilled from the impromptu mud bath I'd received on my way to work, I decided to call a friend who plays the role of protectively indignant well. She had me laughing before I hung up, but the air in my apartment remained quiet and teary. She had cursed Colton and Nancy on my behalf, which I had been avoiding myself. She had cast stones that fell back, weighting my pockets.

My bathroom looks entirely different if you sit on the floor opposite the toilet (I ended up there after kneeling to tighten some loose screws on the toilet paper holder). The efficiently packed porcelain toilet and bath took on queer geometry from a cat's eye view. I'd noticed this before, when I knelt retching over the toilet bowl, but had attributed the sense of disorientation to flu-induced fever and/or drunkenness. This time, the vertigo clearly stemmed from the unfamiliar perspective on the desperately familiar bathroom. I knelt on the bath mat and the fish on the shower curtain began to swim, the showerhead levitating above them. I took off my clothes, sat on top of them, and contemplated the tan-lined body that two people had touched and neither wanted anymore.

I keep a straight razor in a little safety jacket in the pocket of my jeans. I use it at work to cut broken spines off hard covers that need to be sent in for rebinding. It shone quite brightly in the bathroom light. It contrasted with my dull, dry skin. I shaved some fine blonde hairs from my forearm and, mouthing whoosh, I drew the blade across my wrist.

Tell me about this temple of the fifth pillar, Gaia demanded.

So Hanuman spun a tale that wound in seventeen small circles. He told the Gods about the five tall pillars of the temple, the happy faces of the children, and how he ate only mangoes and clouds there and never touched the fields. He concluded saying that he had best return to the temple, it had been long unattended.

Yes, Hanuman, the Gods said, go, tend to your temple, but come back in a fortnight.

The monkey was anxious that no one follow him because he was destined for what he believed to be an imaginary place. When he left the pantheon, he made as though he were heading for the mouth of the cave, and then he jumped. He jumped farther than ever before and higher than ever before, out of the sight of all gods. And, after he flew past the stars in their orbits and the spinning galaxies, Hanuman landed in a curious place.

A place much like the one he had described to his gods.

There were five tall pillars, a basket of mangoes, a field of rice, and a host of worshippers, eager-to-please. Hanuman was terrified! He was caught in a web of his own making! He had forgotten that he too was a god. And when the people bowed before him, and peeled him ripe mangoes, and kissed his hairy toes, the monkey forgot that he was wise and lighthearted and became suddenly foolish and very serious indeed.

In the aftermath of the razor's whoosh there were spatters of blood on the floor and the bath mat, but not as much blood as you might expect. Acting in subliminal cliché, I had slit my wrist in the wrong direction. Also, 'slit' might be slightly overstated. Let's call the wound slightly deeper than a paper cut but still the most terrifying thing I've ever seen. The blood seeped out in a row of beads that actually rolled down my arm when I raised my hand. I screamed. I dropped the stupid razor into the toilet bowl and clenched my wrist with my other hand. What was I supposed to do? It sounded like my neighbours were home, moving around in the apartment next door, but I was too naked to call for help. Normally when I was wounded I'd run the cut under water to clean it and wash off the blood, but I was scared that this would only make me lose more blood and prevent clotting. I have read a lot of murder mysteries. A lot of gang trash thrillers too. I didn't want to die like a washed-up informant. I tried applying pressure, pressing my life back in, but blood seeped up, pushing red daisies through my bracelet of wadded toilet paper.

Hanuman jumped as far as he could and came only halfway back to the pantheon. He jumped again and reached only half that distance. However close he came, there was always another length between him and the Gods and he cried for them the way a child does for its mother, the way the waves do for the wind.

A fortnight passed, two weeks, fourteen days, more hours than a frightened monkey jumping through ether can count to, but at long last Hanuman's lips touched Krishna's smooth blue feet.

I went to the temple of the five pillars! Hanuman cried. It was huge! It was scary! There were five giant sandstone pillars crowded against the edge of time! And this time, Lords, this time, Sirs and Madams, I swear that I ate nothing!

Where is this place? the Gods asked.

A far jump away was as all Hanuman could tell them.

And how would we know it if we saw it? the Gods asked.

The five pillars, Hanuman said, there is nothing else like them in the world!

Calm down little monkey, said the Man in the Yellow Hat, picking Hanuman up in his arms. He showed the monkey his hand. There was a cut on his ring finger, no larger than a paper cut, and no deeper, and quietly Shakyamunii asked, did the pillars look anything like this?

And the monkey's face looked very like a man's.

Then when Odin laughed, and Jesus winked and shook his head, and Allah kissed the monkey's forehead, Hanuman became lighthearted again and very, very wise. Much, much wiser than before.

The bleeding did kind of stop after I wrapped the toilet paper bandage in duct tape. But I was scared to take the duct tape off and let my life gush out of me. I pulled on some clothes and walked twelve blocks to St. Andrew's Emergency. I told them that I was climbing around in my kitchen to reach some high cupboards and fell on a paring knife. They may have believed me. They offered me water and salty crackers. I didn't need stitches. A nurse wrapped my wrist in placating gauze and sent me on my way. I walked home dazed, jumpy, and puddle shy, then wrapped the gauze in a more reliable bracelet of ducttape and slept like a stone. This morning, I woke up and went to work as usual, minus my razor blade and wristwatch. I left work at five and ate a honey ham, cream cheese, and bean sprout pita wrap at Carol's Cafe. In the eclectic audience of Ears to Hear, I felt lucky for the first time in days. Protected by a god wise enough to imagine the mistakes of men, wily enough to think up duct tape.

Gustav finished to a round of applause, bowed, and moved off to make space for a lady named Krystal Ball and her collection of rawhide drums. I nodded and smiled, it was God, he was great — then I ducked out of my hippie tablemate's questions about my faux German mother's feelings regarding neo-Naziism by way of some people I had to meet. Me and these fictitious people will go shopping tomorrow. Tonight we're calling Nancy. I'll see if she knows yet what colour of dress, what kind of dress, she's going to make me wear.

Open Land

WHAT HE WANTED WAS TO RUN. Forwards. Through to the cold openness of the field where his cousins and uncle would be waiting, breath and exhaust swirling above the snowmobiles. Sparked engines humming. Dean would pound his boots over the tread lines in the snow, rush the pull of the machines, and fly through the brightness of a winter morning. The fence posts would brighten, one after another, in the frosted spillway of the rising sun.

Christmas Eve there was a storm warning, heavy flurries forecast to last a day, so Dean walked to Safeway for supplies. A squash, hot chocolate mix, Hawkins Cheezies, coffee beans, granola, yogurt, and a bag of mandarin oranges that froze on the walk back and thawed to mush. Angela stayed on the couch at home, eyes raw and red because she'd been crying in front of Christmas specials all afternoon, and because she was somewhat allergic to the cat she'd insisted on bringing back from the farm. When she bent over the oven to roll the squash her face caught a faint bit of light, just enough to make the red moons beside her nostrils show. She settled back on the couch, hunkered like a snow bank under a white afghan, pure, level, eco-holier than thou.

Dean had agreed to the boycott of Christmas lights because Angela spouted longer if you argued, but mainly because he hadn't been that eager to climb a ladder at minus thirty degrees

Celsius — either way, the decree had left their condo gloomy. When he tromped home with their groceries the neighbour's LEDs twinkled brightly through snow hanging over their eaves. His aunt and uncle at the farm made a point of putting up enough lights that they could be seen from the highway, a bubble of cheer for the long-haul truckers at night. No lights, no gifts, Angela seemed to be opting out of 'consumerism' and human kindness in one swoop. Yet, she sobbed over *It's a Wonderful Life*, enveloped by her afghan, firm in her insistence that their thermostat remain in the lower teens.

Waiting for dinner, Dean made them each a hot chocolate with Irish cream and Angela revived over hers briefly. She picked out the marshmallows and disgorged interesting facts about furnace efficiency, sea otters, and global warming while George Bailey gathered his family for carols on the TV behind her.

(C4.89) *The lovers exhaled at exactly the same time. The grass fell away beside them, trailing onto a bird printed strand that lapped into the water. She was naked, pink and white, and her hair sand coloured. He curled around her body, hung with half-removed clothing. The blond fur of his belly tickled her back and he cupped the swell of her left breast with his right hand. And then the sun fell between them, glinting gold on the edges of her scales . . . as their bodies slipped apart.*

Or maybe . . . the moon was broken in the waves that lapped near their feet.

In bed early on Christmas night, tangled in spent sheets, Dean attempted writerly alchemy. To rise above indigestion from the fibrous squash, and his current conditions, which saw Angela committing treason on the phone in the bathroom. She was perched on the counter among her raw earth beauty products, trimming her toenails into the sink, and telling her mom about his 'prize'.

"What is this award, anyway," she'd asked when he'd called her at work to tell her about it. "I've never heard of it — who's it from?"

An Internet fan site. He'd been posting installments live and won a reader's choice award. Also, most comments. It *was* flattering, but first she'd blown the whole thing out of proportion, and now she was backtracking and slamming his prize every time she talked to their family and friends. No, it didn't mean the book was getting publication. He hadn't won anything but a trophy icon. "And get this," she was giggling, "it flashes!"

Whatever.

It was tacky, but he had fans, perhaps not so much due to his fine writing as to a topical stroke of luck that Xaydin's anti-terror policy mirrored that of G.W. Bush, USA. The humans, you see, had launched UV reflecting satellites to combat global warming (Angela liked that), but the Xaydin mistook them for laser focusing units. SETI's reiterated strings of prime numbers, beamed through space to signal earthly intelligence, had been misread as intergalactic spam. A mathematical blind. Dean's final sentence of the love scene between Xaydin math dog, Jxling, and his fishy girlfriend was meant to both finish the chapter, round it out, and lead to the impending war. You couldn't use 'lapped' twice in a paragraph, so their bodies had to *slip apart*. That could also foreshadow that Jxling would not come home. Maybe they could *roll apart*. Who flushes the toilet on the phone?

The note Angela left on Dean's dresser when she left for work New Year's morning contained three hugs and four kisses as well as a snippet from a Rilke poem: *on a night like this, all cities are alike* . . . She finished, *Dean this is just so good. Imagine, you could write a book just like this. Why not?*

Where did she get the impression that he wrote poetry? That he could or would breathe universality into a thunderstorm? Assuming that was what this Rilke poem was about. Trust Angela to pull the seldom-used English degree out. Dean had penned a lot of storms, to highlight plot, pivotal dark and stormy astral nights . . . *Jxling had never felt wind drive so fiercely. It whipped his small craft, spears of rain driving hard into the view screen. A ruffle of wind through his fur was his only warning . . .* that shit was breaking apart.

It wasn't until after the 'award' that Angela had bothered to read the entirety of Dean's saga. She deemed it 'kind of' dramatic. In the first chapter there were people puking all over the place on sight of hideous alien appendages, but Dean had been proud of the description of a soldier's blood flowing from his blasted open side and pointed her to it. The guy was writhing in agony but with it enough to watch a red rivulet run across a reflective titanium floor to merge with a wounded Xaydin soldier's bilious green excretions. On Earth, far below the dying soldiers (who were on a space station), the fuel cell of the first Xaydin spacecraft brought down by anti-aircraft missiles began, slowly but surely, to leak into the Ganges. The idea was that it would cause all kinds of radioactive mutations, but Angela focused on the fuel cell. Was it a green-alternative?

What Dean wanted was to fly over the snow. Not even driving, just riding, gripping someone equally wild for speed. He wanted open land, gasoline combusting, and the slap of wind hard on his cheek.

At the farm there was an electric well in the yard. It gargled and droned periodically throughout the day as Faith set the line pumping. They had a slough on their land but it was salty, useless for watering cows. The slough's edge was a saggy lip of mud, lapped by a ring of salt at the water's margin, which Dean and Jason, the cousin nearest his age, mined for birds. Coyote-, farm cat-, or simply, winter-killed, their mummified bodies appeared every spring. Feathers and snow mould formed wreaths around headless torsos, wires of muscle glittered, rimed by crystals of salt wicked up from the mud. Dean and Jason knelt before these small and beautiful horrors, to pry loose their wishbones. Aunt Faith hung them on the dial of her oven timer to dry.

Cross arms, wish hard, and pull. Bone cracks, splinters fly, and you are left holding twigs. The smallest hollow of a bird and if the bridge of the breastbone stays in your hand you have it. Your wish. The trick always being, before you close your eyes, before you pull, to know what to ask for.

With Angela back at work, mediating message boards for the PC Police, Dean was meant to focus. To wrap the war up, four hundred pages deep. He couldn't get past the backstory and the memory of himself, no more than six or seven, skipping through his aunt's farmyard in green rubber boots. They made happy face footprints. He had been stomping, splashing happiness into the mud, bird bits aloft in a pincer grip.

Angela had risen early, supposedly leaving Dean to sleep in but hitting snooze on the alarm so many times that it would have been impossible for him to linger in anything resembling quality rest. When she came out of the shower, cranky about the morning shift, he complained that he had nothing to wish on. Elaborated that they had nothing to wish on. Sleep-fuddled, he was speaking literally. They'd had squash for Christmas, no bones between them. He offered, to her offended tears, explanation and the image of salt crystals, glittering along a magpie's ribcage. She wouldn't bite.

Angela had actually suggested a visit to the farm before Christmas. Dean had rhapsodized the cold brightness of winter out there, the land open to the wind, scoured by snow. She wanted to go, claiming to love Faith and her energy, but the Christmas kitsch would have killed her. And Dean had imagined the notes too clearly. A dog-eared Sharon Butala appearing when they came home. Folded pages, and Angela's sticky note, post scripted *xo*. *These descriptions of the sky. Of the land. You could write this, how the sky and the long view of the land shaped, expanded, your voice.* Yes, well, he'd hid in his cousin's closet reading nothing but comics the first time they sent him to the farm on his own. Dean had countered Angela with a two-star resort trip to Mexico, tickets cheap on a last minute deal. Angela wavered, between the sun, the ocean, and the sheer quantity of oil consumed by commercial jets. She had wavered.

On a night like this all cities are alike/ with cloud-flags hung/ the banners by the storm are flung/ torn out like hair/ in any country anywhere/ whose boundaries and rivers are uncertain . . . Angela, I take you everywhere. I don't ignore your wishes for my writing, you're always there, I find your hairs in my butt when I shower, x D. It was true, though perhaps he didn't need to have left the note sitting out on the kitchen island. When, yes, he did know she had friends coming over after work. Did it make her look stupid? He supposed it did. Her hair was long and smooth and always falling out, getting tangled in the folds of their pillows and sheets and bodies. He had intended the note only for her.

(C19.257) There was a stillness that Khazi visited, when he knelt beside the Xaydin nucleo-mines. When he held his knife against their casings. It silenced the story of his sister who was almost born and might have been if the bomb hadn't pitched his mother from the side of the dam. But it could not swallow the idea of that field beneath the dam, alive with crickets, flooded in violence. Nor the idea of a lake, thick with fish, made to disappear by a single strike of the Xaydins' beam.
"Out go the lights," he whispered, always, as he slid his knife in.

By the end, Earth was meant to be entering a post-Xaydin dystopian era. The lake had been drained when the dam blew apart, but then the satellites launched to trap Xaydin-sourced radiation went rogue, ravaging and remagnetizing virtually all compu-tech, including the remote drones. It was catastrophic, but worked to Earth's advantage in the end, crippling the Xaydin communication system. In a breath of respite, the Fisher people were meant to cobble the dam back together. In the sunken field, a new lake's surface was meant to be swelling, punctuated by tips of marsh grass rising in hummocks along its edge. The children were sent out, many of them into the sun for the first time, to mine the field for salvageable scrap in the water's advance. They scrambled, mud streaked, stumbling over their prizes, the detritus of war. Heads level with drowning grass, the wind would tousle hummocks and children alike.

Initiating the dare that sent Dean into the slough after a falcon that appeared to have dropped dead on the spring ice, cousin Jason shared a story about a horse floundering to death as salt crystals sliced its tendons — an exaggeration Dean's uncle later refuted.

When Dean crossed, on snowshoes, from the muddy lip of the slough to the salt pan that hovered, inches below the surface of the water, he had — wind and waves on every side — been flying through fear towards the bird on the ice. Miraculous, until the pan broke through. And then, despite padded track pants, a knife-edge of salt sliced Dean's calf. His shin was crosshatched as he thrashed his leg backwards and forwards, floundering down. It was only a metre deep where Dean went through, but the water was icy cold and its clear surface billowed suddenly with blackness. Decaying insects, dead things, swelled up from the underbelly of the slough.

The detail made no sense for the book, but Dean wanted the Fisher-children's legs netted by scars like his. Luck can carry you only so far, only so many times, and by the end of his book everyone had to know that.

Frustrating as it had been to concentrate through Christmas specials and Angela's intentions for his social life, Dean had more time for writing over the holidays than he would now until summer. He had returned dutifully to a business college's tech support office. The job had required a degree and familiarity with diverse software, but Dean seemed, most often, to coach the college's instructors in the fine arts of smart boards and downloading pictures of their grandchildren. His Xaydin Saga comments fell off. His holiday installments had been rambling, and he knew that, working backstory. Angela tried, and Dean did notice that she was trying, to cheer him up. She bumped the thermostat up by a degree for the peak TV window and pitched staying in with hockey for a Saturday night date. He threw his legs over her on the couch and she moved her fingers over the criss-crossed scars on his calves, light, ticklish.

"This is nice," she offered. It was not drinks with friends, a political movie, or a concert — not even a coffee and bookstore tour. It was hockey, not-her-favourite-thing. Dean suspected that he had been immobilized for a talk. That if he were to turn his face away from the hockey game, which was not–particularly–his-thing either, she would offer up a ready can of worms. Nice.

Her fingers started and paused with her thoughts but before she could comment — on the Mountain Dew bottles accumulating in the rear entry, the ridiculous violence of sport, or the inefficiency of an ice rink in Florida — Dean made her jump. Swearing, loudly, at a penalty call.

He had not told her about the underside of the saltpan when he introduced her to the farm in the summer, though he had walked her down to the slough and told her about Jason's dare. Omitting the horror of the fetid black mud sliding through his bloody wounds, and the cold sting when Faith hosed him off in the barn beside the winter calves, it was a funny story. Omitting

Open Land

Dean's retaliation which saw Jason's comic books swell apart in the turgid water — Angela would not like that part of the story. But the story is not about what Angela would like.

As the hockey game proceeded to overtime, she turned and stretched out, nestling between the back of the couch and Dean's legs, her head on his lap.

"You can't put everything in it," she'd said briefly, of the book, between periods.

Dean pocketed this note before leaving: *Sorry I didn't clean the cat puke off the couch before your friends came over. I really forgot. Not to belabour the point, but you are the one who left the butter sitting out. Don't forget to feed him while I'm away, xox D.* He is sorry, later, not to have left an alternate, nicer, note. He read something once about two people, metaphorical rocks, rubbing each other, tumbling into jewels — maybe it was in one of her collected books. He wishes that he could have written something in that vein for her. Or at least that he had left an *I'll be back*, which of course he would. He is sorry also, in having left for the farm directly from work, not to have taken Angela's note with him. He can't remember all of it, except that it demanded an apology regarding the puke. Angela was, for this New Year, attempting directness and clarity.

On the highway Dean saw a billboard, dated by the passage of the holidays and peeling already: *Has your lady been bad? Buy her a billion-year-old lump of coal for Christmas! Gold, white gold, and platinum settings. Sergeant's Diamonds, five minutes away on Highway 11.* A ring wouldn't work but, for clarity, what Dean wanted between them was for Angela's pinched, critical face to change just once like Faith's. Opening, delighted by his offerings. Faith mentioned nothing else, not the mud on her floor or the muck on her nephew, until she had rinsed his wishbones in her kitchen sink.

(C37.589) There had been a stillness in the field, which as a child Khazi imagined was the same stillness that water had, underneath. At first, the land gave up mysterious glimpses of things that should have been underwater. Things that someone, sometime, threw out into sparkling waves. Broken pottery, a useless single shoe, an old memory drive. When the grass got longer, and dryer, the land's imagination changed. Khazi's mother went to pick yellow flowers and red samphire from the crescent where salt leached up near what used to be the shore of the sometimes lake.

The missive Angela posted to Dean's Facebook wall just said that she missed him, and that he should say 'hi' to his aunt Faith and to uncle Dave. To enjoy his time back home. But the farm had always been a refuge. Temporary. He has no doubt that his aunt fostered him with love but support cheques from his overwhelmed parents had been involved. Dean is sure that Angela has not forgotten his missed apology. So her plain good wishes, absent of anger, must have been forwarded in truce. This or the apt assumption that Faith would be at his shoulder when he sat before her office computer.

(C38.600) Khazi wondered if, after the mines were cleared, people would come back to the empty houses. It was an improbable way to restock the fishery but what Khazi imagined was the Fisher people cheering as a net opened — a war ended — and from a hovering freight cruiser their newly treaty-ized allies dropped silver fish, one by one, flashing and flipping . . .

He ran back through time, through the tall, arcing grasses of the emptied field to the shore of the lake that had been and would be. No matter the height of the sun, its light would be caught on the water. The casing pulsed against his knife, but Khazi never knew what hit him.

The road in to the farm nearly rocked the axle out of Dean's car. Soon after he turned off the grid his stereo started skipping, then ate the CD so he couldn't shut it off. He had to stop his car to silence a repetitive too quick beat of 'do-to-to-to-to-to-to'. The snow was crisp, gravelly stuff that crunched when he restarted. The shocks groaned as the car's underside grazed the median of a trail that nothing but snowmobiles had evidently used since the latest dump. The white land felt beautifully familiar, featureless except for this track and the loops where kids had off-roaded beside it, charging up and down through the blue shadows that marked dips and swells in the snow. The outline of the farm on the horizon was the same, the barn, the outbuildings, and the house. This had always been the approach, so Dean was surprised, pulling into the circle of buildings, to see a ploughed drive heading off in the other direction.

They would have heard his car approaching, but it was manners here to wait for a knock, so Dean parked and began walking towards the front of the house. He caught himself before the porch, because knocking would have been wrong. Family was meant to scrape their boots and bang in; they'd always told him that. But barging into the kitchen felt awkward too, when Faith materialized from the hall that led to the front room.

"Here's Dean!" she shouted, holding him back to see his face. She had dyed and cut her hair in the oddly aging manner of women trying to look young. Uncle Dave, emerging from the TV room, was thinner and shorter than Dean remembered. They seemed happy to see him, if somewhat amused.

"So, here's Dean," Dave echoed, "I guess he doesn't know we got a road up the west drive, does he?"

"I guess he doesn't," Faith agreed.

"I didn't know that," Dean said. "Nope."

"It was here last time you were," Dave said.

"Was it really?" Had Angela been driving?

"You're lucky you didn't get stuck."

"Well — winter tires."

"You'll have wrecked the track."

Dean had forgotten about braking suddenly for frozen ruts. Slamming against his cousin's back, the windproof shell of his suit crinkling, brittle. The risk, at speed of the snowmobile overturning was too great.

"The Drummond boys have been running out that way," Uncle Dan added.

Then Faith, smiling, "Ah well."

That terseness caught it right. It'd been done. They set in to quizzing him about work, and Angela's work, and the nuisance cat they'd taken home in the summer after Dan's threat to drop it in a field for the coyotes. It had been a nuisance in the dairy. It was a nuisance in the condo. Dean really should have made sure that Angela knew to go home to feed it. Desmond was liable to spray when offended, and Dean thought of calling Angela at work, to minimize damage, but Faith had dinner ready to serve in a kitchen made both quaint and creepy by an overabundance of desiccated avian collarbones.

Jason and his older brother had been in Afghanistan for Christmas, their sister Karen had gone to Edmonton with her husband's family, and Dave and Faith had been invited out for New Year's. Wishes were stockpiling, with three grandchildren now keen on collecting the bones. They'd been sending them in the mail. It had been a while since they'd had a proper reunion to pull them at.

"Too long," Dean's aunt and uncle said, words rolling in practiced unison. Dean smiled.

"But," Faith scolded, "anyone else we'd expect a visit from would know perfectly well how to come home."

Mandala

ONE OF MY FIRST MEMORIES IS of my mother explaining where she planned to get me a little sister from. I was aghast, picturing a vagina no larger than the slit at the end of my penis, a baby squeezed out like toothpaste from a tube, and my mother deflated afterwards, shriveled and hollow. These misconceptions were graphically corrected when she popped my sister out onto the kitchen linoleum with three ground-shaking contractions, and remained strong enough to shout me into telephoning her parents. I padded importantly to the phone in my parents' room for that call, awed by my unsupervised responsibility. The part of her sex-ed lecture that stuck with me later was the contribution of the father. Contrary to the popular belief of four-year-olds, that mothers made babies solo, I knew that fathers provided the blueprints. Via penis delivery.

The best approach with grizzly bears is to back away slowly while making a lot of noise. If they do charge, you should play dead while they paw you and hopefully do not eat you. If the bear is black, you should try to back away slowly while making a lot of noise. However, if a black bear charges you, you should fight back with great vigor, poking them in the eye if possible. If you have ever been faced by an angry bear, you know how hard this advice is to follow. Instinctively, the human creature runs away, gasping and squealing in anticipation of death. My sister, faced with a bear that appeared to be both black and brown, ran screaming. She was an avid believer in anything read or read to her, but only three, with little life experience. Little enough to mistake a slobbering Saint Bernard for a rabid bear. She was embarrassed by our father's laughter. I was humiliated for her — she, my mother and me being the proud breed of know-it-all that preferred errors of fact or judgment to be ignored quietly. Not recounted delightedly by my father to the owner of the Saint Bernard, the woman walking by who was flustered by Xanthe's screaming, or the zit-ridden Dickee Dee boy.

I was in grade three (by which time grades had replaced years in my estimation of maturity) when my father and I went to Ikea. We were consciously disobeying my mother who thought it was just plain silly to buy a new table when a second hand table could be covered in a tablecloth and look just as nice. At least, I was consciously disobeying my mother, and so nauseated by guilt that I threw up the hot dog my father had bought as a treat. My father had enjoyed shopping with a child, manoeuvering our cart in and out of other family units, picking out surprise items for an imaginary wife and daughter who would enjoy them.

My mother died when I was almost ten and Xanthe barely five; she was thirty-three. She died of blood poisoning after cutting her hand on a knife that had been left unwashed for three days after being used to fillet a fish, in a Buddhist nunnery in Thalot, India. I'm not kidding. It's in Ladakh, the northernmost province of India, deep in the Indian Himalayas. She was away from Western medicine and a Tibetan herbalist tried various remedies and bloodlettings but what she needed was a heavy dose of antibiotics and maybe a blood transfusion.

Mandela

We stayed at the nunnery for a week after her death, until the cook found Western tourists he deemed respectable enough to help us track down our father. His choices included hippies, Israeli students revelling in their freedom from mandatory military duty, and a few earnest mountaineers lying prone with altitude sickness while they dreamt of mastering windy passes with trains of yaks. The Buddhists gave us to Rick and Leonard.

Assembling a table from Ikea requires no great genius. But Xanthe and I rarely made crafts or collections or experiments that were not accompanied by extensive instructions — *Mr. Dressup's Rainy Day Parade, Dr. Zed's Amazing Experiments, A Child's Book of Bug Collection, Simon and Schuster's Guide to Rocks and Minerals, Yama Origami*. Xanthe read aloud while I assembled, ordered, labelled, or folded, and considered the results hers. Her ability to read (mastered by age two-and-a-half) was her greatest pride, a satisfaction to my mother and I who had read her alphabet books in the womb, an astonishment to my father (and probably the rest of the family, town, world). There are no written instructions for assembly of an Ikea table. Clutching an unappreciated gift of a green and yellow pillow (which to Dad's credit did match her comforter), Xanthe watched with trepidation as my father began screwing and assembling without even glancing at instructions. I peered over her shoulder with interest. It seemed blueprints were not necessary to construction. My mother came home. She was steely silent about the table in her kitchen, and breathed shortly and dismissively as my father gestured towards a pair of candles and a set of picture frames. Xanthe and I followed my mother to her room — rewarded by her confidences, and justified in disapproving our father's extravagances.

I don't know why the cook picked men to take care of Xanthe and me. Maybe this is a Western prejudice, but were I in his position, I would have petitioned the first neatly dressed woman I saw. Maybe he thought a woman would remind us painfully of our mother? Maybe he thought we should get used to men if we were going to live with our father? Maybe they were the only strong English speakers he could find and he really wanted to get rid of us.

Bears and dogs are actually closely related in a phylogenetic sense, my mother explained over the rhythm of our tooth brushing. They share a common ancestor that looked something like a wolverine. The divergence probably began by geographic separation, after which the two populations began to evolve in response to different environmental stresses. Likely, dogs evolved in a place where food was scarce and teamwork and agility necessary to survival. Bears, which lead solitary and relatively sedentary lives, evolved in more plentiful environments. We, her children, nodded sagely while we brushed, coordinating brush stroke and head movement. Xanthe was placated, honour restored. My mother's omniscience was confirmed.

If my father, who had to be told that Dylan Thomas died from alcohol, and furthermore ignored this fact and brazenly sipped at a beer with dinner on Fridays, could assemble a table without instructions, I was sure my mother could build babies without instructions from him.

Suddenly she was dead, and Rick was incredibly tall and old. With hindsight, he was five foot, seven inches and only twenty-three. But those Northern Indian Tibetan types were short little people, and the nuns with their shaved heads tended to look younger than they were. Rick was terrified by the idea of taking on diarrhea-ridden children, but saw no better option for us. He was also relieved that taking us on necessitated abandoning Leonard's two-month high-altitude embolism-taunting trek schedule.

Mandela

My father left us on a Tuesday and Xanthe and I didn't realize until Thursday. My mother knew of course, but waited until we noticed. She minimized the importance of his disappearance. Life changed very little for me. I sat in Mrs. Kleason's classroom much as before, but with the novelty of being the child of a single parent, and enjoyed the curiosity of my classmates. I was tempted to tell stories featuring violent parental fighting, thrown dishes, and high courtroom drama. I bit my creative tongue and found that silence added to my classroom mystique. What did change was that my mother no longer felt free to pursue her self-directed education, or Xanthe's. We would not be beholden to HIM. Xanthe was enrolled in a Montessori preschool while my mother became a research assistant to Dr. Levin, a professor of religious studies.

I identified Leonard as what my mother called a pothead. But he dressed well and had clean smelling hair, despite its being knotted in dreads. I could see why the cook had chosen him. He looked rich. Very geared up in synthetic mountaineering apparel. Not a hippie stuck in India because he was out of money for the flight home.

Dr. Levin arranged funding for my mother to pursue a doctoral thesis. She was exploring the contrasts between ideal and actualized religion — with a focus on the actualization of Buddhism in different ecological and economic environments. This began with a month spent at the Mt. Tuam Monastery on Salt Spring Island. We were the only children present. Xanthe, at four, haloed by blonde curls and studiously introspective, was an immediate darling of the monks. I spent my time on verdant hill slopes, taunting sheep under the guise of shepherding.

We arrived in Delhi just before the monsoon season and withered immediately in the heat. My mother did not approve of man-powered rickshaws and did a lot of walking carrying a hot and sweaty Xanthe and dragging me by the hand. I was dizzied by Delhi. It was a swarm of heat and exhaust. The bottom of my feet sweated and my heels slid wetly out of my sandals with every step. We fascinated and were touched by merchants, businessmen, peddlers, and lepers. My mother was fascinated by them, oblivious to the knots of pity and disgust that writhed in me.

A whole family drove by our bus on a scooter.

My mother held Xanthe's head while she puked out the window — and a man drove by on a scooter, his son gripped between his knees on the running board, his wife behind him holding an infant, and another boy behind her, gripping her sari with monkey fists. They flew by the bus, heads turning in unison to watch my sister's puckered face.

Trees and stones seemed more real. I rolled a pebble back and forth over the crest of my knee while Rick and Leonard discussed whether to keep us. Plan B would have been to hand us over to a military base, and the military was busy enough with Sikh–Hindu tensions and periodic border skirmishes with Pakistan. They decided to take us to Delhi where we could be turned over to the Canadian Embassy. I knew the role of an embassy. I may even have known the address of the embassy, that being the sort of tangible information I tended to file away. But I was suddenly aware that I had no idea what an Embassy was — a building? A group of people? Could it be a machine?

Rick turned his back to Leonard and I and threw a pebble he'd been palming over the balcony of the nunnery, a long graceful arc that ended whooshing into a field of green wheat. I leapt up beside him and threw my pebble, a short wobbling cosine that bounced back at me from the balcony railing. Rick swooped me up in tanned arms. The scruffy stubble of his chin scraped my forehead, his calloused fingers dug into my left arm and thigh, and he swung me over the edge of the balcony after his pebble.

I hovered between sky and wheat, long enough for a fearful gasp and the beginning of wonder.

And then he swung me back, a stiff, almost ten year old boomerang.

Leonard was a reluctant babysitter throughout, but a responsible one. First off, he talked a pharmacy into giving us Flagyl and relieved Xanthe and me of our dehydrating giardiasis. I remember my first unafflicted morning clearly. We had stopped at a tent camp overnight on a three-day bus trip out of the mountains and I woke up before anyone else. My stomach did not hurt, and sitting up did not produce gassy rumblings. I slipped out from a cozy position between Rick and Xanthe and ventured out of the tent. I was very small and stood in the middle of a bone dry crater-like sedimentary basin. We had driven through this same landscape with my mother a month ago, but I was seeing it for the first time. She left a huge void in my psyche and five a.m. light and crumbling mountain passes were filtering into it. I stumbled away from the circle of tents, squatted in full view of anything watching, and shat. A real solid BM.

I was reluctant to admit to myself that Rick was better at taking care of Xanthe than either my mother or I. He was unflustered by vomit and unanswerable questions and firmly disinterested in encouraging her meditation. Having asked for a book to read and being told that Milan Kundera was too grown up for her, Xanthe tried tearfully to meditate on a bus ride. I had defected to the Rick and Leonard camp of rough-housing and guffaws. Motion sick, and heartsick, she sought inner resources as our mother and the monks had taught her to do.

Rick's crappy limericks battered at her resolve, his long tanned fingers tickled her sides, he pulled at her toes.

There was a blond girl named Xan-thee
Who tried to be real fan-cy
"I am not!"
There was a wee tyke from Loredo
who longed for a big baked potato
but she had no chive
and began to jive
(a great deal of wriggling ensued as my sister attempted to escape tickling fingers)
Until she turned into a great big tomato!!
Bpppppppppp!!!!!
(A tomato to Rick is a raspberry to most people — which we didn't know then. His lips forming a shuddering, noisy volcano that erupted on your stomach or arm seemed a phenomenon unique to him.) My sister erupted into giggling. Her sunburnt, tear-streaked face turned all smiles.

When they thought I was asleep, nestled between them on the final leg back to Delhi, I listened to what I considered a candid discussion of sex. Leonard was a wandering poet, Rick a sleepy and receptive listener. The sweet smoke of Leonard's pipe wafted above my head. I had come to think of it as incense, no different from the kind my mother burned to centre herself before writing. Learning is opening yourself to the world; writing is opening the world to your thoughts. It requires silence and centering. Leonard was lecturing Rick on technique and timing.

"Sure if she's wet you could dive in" is the phrase I awoke to.

"But you don't want her in her body when you go in, or you in yours. Because the physical touch is one thing, but it's sex without connection unless you're above that. Way above it. You've gotta wait until going into her is the only thing you can do because you're riding a wave that won't stop for a gate. Its birth in reverse — you are diving through a portal into the workshop that is woman, the flower you came out of as pollen; she is a sea you beached yourself out of when you were born — and she is right to be angry at losing you. Because man is a part of woman, man is of woman. So when she lets you back in she's being fucking generous, and you've got to be grateful. Not just horny and hungry but full of worship and thanks. Sex is fucking and it's nothing. You want to make love to a woman. And don't think you need to love her to do that. It's man and woman, not a man, not a woman. If you want Carol bound to you in any way, man, you've got to tie yourself into that love..."

The discussion continued.

I was looking at penis delivery in a very different way. And the idea of putting myself into a woman's body, which I had only vaguely considered before, became suddenly immediate and frightening. Because man was the vulnerable one enveloped in what Leonard described. And I knew about this portal to woman, I had seen one bloody and angry. And my father had entered it. Shivery, guilty of eavesdropping, I coughed and sat up.

At one monastery we visited, my mother explained the scenes in a mandala: All of creation in all of its states in one picture. Birth, growth, work, death, again and again cycling infinite. She tried to key me into the power of life, asking if I remembered the speed of Xanthe's birth — the way she clambered into the world. I was hot, dehydrated, needed a washroom, and dying to escape the heat and expectancy of my mother's body hunching over me. I nodded. She smiled. Because We delivered Xanthe, and We named her. But I was a reluctant conspirator. I could barely remember the birth. I did remember my pleasure at dialing the phone in my parents' room though — previous to that day, I had only pressed individual buttons to hear them beep. And I had done so stealthily, while my mother was in the shower.

Xanthe has turned out normal (ish). She is smart, but I think she would have been so without our early coaching. She is artistic and musical and popular, and these were born in her too. My father, become Dad, sees our mother in her. Tempered. Deeply capable of love. I look more like our dad, and act like him after an adolescence of increasingly conscious mimicry. I catch his expressions in my mouth, his movements in my body. My mother swirls deep, held here, within our lives, mine and Xanthe's.

We drove Rick and Leonard crazy in Delhi. Panicky and frightened of losing our tenuous claim to them, we demanded piggyback rides in forty-degree heat, refused to use the washroom unaccompanied, and begged for song. We took a rickshaw to the Canadian Embassy with their promise to visit us in Canada clenched in our fists.

The last person we expected to find behind the doors of the embassy was our father. Happy to see us but prepared to handle us like stemware. He expected us crippled by loss, or still angry with him for leaving. He stumbled over greetings, apologetic and uncertain what to offer. These restless, shaggy-headed, tanned creatures were not who he remembered his children being. We had succumbed to instinct. In the darknesses of night and stillness we were safekept by strangers who offered nothing but food, humour, and physical presence. Most children are born trusting the constancy of matter, the solidity of their father's chest. They learn to stand beside the tall trunks of their mother's legs. We were born to our father late, free of imagined need.

Traplines

WE MET IN THE BARN. I arrived first and startled a goat whose bell jingled and echoed around the yard. Astrid arrived more stealthily, darting through blue shadows cast where trees intercepted the heavy light of late afternoon. She carried an armload of supplies. A six-litre bucket, scissors, a funnel, and a length of flexible tygon tubing stolen from Art. He used it to do tension exercises. I would use it to steal some gas.

We crept over to the Land Rover and Astrid opened the gas door and unscrewed the cap while I cut the tubing to an appropriate length. She squatted nervously beside me as I inserted the tubing and sucked. I got a mouthful of gasoline, but the tube drew the gas up okay.

"Is it working?" She whispered.

I nodded, spat, and spat, and spat. We transferred six-and-a-half buckets of gas between the cars, then stood for a moment between them. I spat again.

"Do you smell us?" Astrid asked, frowning.

I sniffed. I couldn't smell us. I couldn't smell the barn either. Where was the goat, hay, chicken shit smell?

"I can't smell *anything*," she puzzled, wide-eyed.

We had spilled that much gas. In the hay, on our pants, on my chin. It glistened on the side of the Land Rover and made two dark stains on the green tarp that hung over the little red Ford Escort.

"No smoking," Astrid whispered.

"None," I agreed, shaky with fumes.

"Sex?" She asked.

"Now?"

She hid the bucket, funnel, and tubing under the water trough and poked my stomach, "A reason for why we've been gone."

I didn't get it till she tugged her shirt out of her pants. She pinched her cheeks red, bit her lips, and shook some hair loose from her ponytail. I wiped my hands and face on a goat blanket and we rubbed ourselves with scent-masking goat shit before we rushed through the empty kitchen to the shower.

We planned to leave at midnight. The stroke of twelve. April twenty-third. I was quivering with excitement as I towelled off, a fume-high farm kid promised a trip to a real live city.

For a last event at Hadit's Wood, Andre's dream-telling that night wasn't so bad. The sun bowed out pretty spectacularly and Andre stood spotlit by the campfire against a backdrop of trees. A column of smoke was funnelling toward for the poor guy's eyes and they teared as he read a passage he'd chosen from a book of Wiccan verse.

... 'Do what though wilt' is to bid the Stars to shine,
Vines to bear fruit,
Water to seek its level;
Man is the only being in Nature
that has striven to set himself at odds with himself

Too true, I thought, watching Andre's hungry body sway on thin legs.

Go amongst Nature, a part of it, an it harm none, do what thou wilt ...

The firelit faces of the Hadit's Wood brethren nodded, smiling with affection for Andre. The wind changed direction, delivering his eyes from the smoke. "I have seen a vision," he said, "and it is writ in the book of light to be read seven years hence."

We clapped politely.

"Though I shall not tell you the vision, I shall tell you its body and truth: no cold force of practicality, no two particles circling their electromagnetic tracks, could ever, like, generate the celebration of contradiction, rationality and irrationality, beauty and ugliness, creativity and destructiveness that is embodied in the nature of man."

This was some kind of statement of theism — affirmation of a creative and purposeful spirit. I felt something shift between my skull and scalp as Andre read these words. The words felt true, but at the same time, they weren't anything Andre would have written himself. If he had embraced the sentiment on his own he would have said there's a God, there's no other reason for fuckers like us to exist — something in that vein. I wanted to take Remi's words and tongue out of Andre's mouth. I wanted to take him with me away from Hadit's Wood and felt suddenly powerful in the knowledge that I had the ability to do it. I would take Andre along on our escape if he wanted me to.

I'm not sure what went wrong.

I drank a lot that night, keeping Andre company as he scarfed down stew and his own scotch-enhanced honey mead. I heaved him into his top bunk, thinking, he's way too drunk to take right now, but I'll come back for him. I'll come back with the RCMP and prove there's no way he's a day over sixteen and that Remi's been corrupting youth or something. There had to be a charge like that, or brainwashing maybe. I went to brush my teeth in the bathroom, then tucked the toothbrush into my pocket for the escape in such an awkward way that Remi commented on it when he waylaid me in the hall. I tried to slip past him but he sagged against the wall, blocking my way.

"Were you to bed?"

"Yeah," I nodded, a little dizzy, a little drunk.

"We'll talk first."

"Oh," I groaned, "I'm tired."

He waved a palm in my face, grabbed my arm, and pulled me down the stairs to his office.

"P.D., I have an issue for you," he said. We were sitting in ancient armchairs, our knees inches away from touching. The desk lamp was shining a halogen halo around Remi's head. I held onto my toothbrush and tried not to look at the empty tack where the car keys usually hung on the bulletin board beside me.

"Yes," I prompted, squinting.

"Andre," Remi said, then bit his lip.

"Whaddabout him?" I asked, relieved that it didn't seem to be about me.

"He saw nothing." Remi's eyes were wide, dark, and drunk too. I tried to be surprised. I squinted, I shook my head.

"Not one thing," Remi elaborated, then he babbled on. Was it his, Remi's, fault? Was the Hadit's Wood dream quest procedure flawed? Was Andre a human specimen of great rarity, a true empty vessel?

"I dunno," was my contribution.

He kept going but I didn't follow.

I, the woozy oracle, coughed, rubbed my face, and even pretended to fall asleep a couple of times.

" . . . and you! You are empty too, will you see nothing for me?"

I shrugged, but I went from tired to alert and paranoid. Had Remi's psychic feelers intuited my plan to escape? Was he about to call me Dustin to see how I'd react? I almost wanted him to. Astrid hadn't even used my name yet. Were they going to keep me? Kill me? Bury me in a pit with Helen? The bones! Had I dreamt or remembered the bones? A tiny animal or the end of Helen's fingers, reaching up from her grave in the compost heap to warn me into silence? I think I whimpered. Helen's fingers reaching up through the heavy weight of dirt and cabbage pressing down on her, weighing down on me. I whimpered and fell asleep. In a chair opposite Remi the inquisitor, on the eve of my anticipated departure, I tripped into sleep and woke to a tongue in my ear, a brush of stubble across my cheek.

"Ah!" I started, and was saved by the sound of an engine revving to life. Remi frowned, raised inquisitive eyebrows, and darted out of the room. I rubbed my thighs, trying to dispel the lingering feeling of Remi's hand on my knee, and it took me a minute to realize what I had heard. An engine coming to life, the crunch and spin of tires on gravel. By the time I got outside, my escape was reduced to a dull hum between distant trees and a low puff of dust above the road.

Remi was closer to tears than anger.

"Who was that?" I asked.

He shook his head and brushed by me into the house. He checked the beds. Lights came on in the wing with the bedrooms, the baby wailed. I watched from behind the woodpile. I had been late to meet her and Astrid had left without me. There was no gas left in the Land Rover, and there wasn't enough snow left to follow her on the snowmobile.

I should have gone back into the house and played dumb and worried. Once she reached a city, Astrid might have reported my whereabouts to the police who would then find my family. An RCMP cruiser might have pulled into the commune one day asking for Dustin McKeowan. But I didn't go back into the house to wait for anything like that to happen. The idea of someone waiting for me would not leave. She walked ahead of me into the woods and I followed, stumbling to sleep in darkening woods where tiny pockets of snow lingered in deep shadow. I blew on my hands to warm them, pulled them into my sleeves, and tucked myself into the kind of drunk and dreamless sleep that time has no place in or claim to.

Astrid's birthday had been in December. She turned thirty-seven, but I was the only one who knew that. We gathered around a table in the dining hall, greedy for iced corn cakes, but before we ate we held hands and sang: *Happy birthday to you, happy birthday to you, happy birthday dear Astrid . . .*

Astrid blew out a fat storm candle Dawn pinioned one of the cakes with, and closed her eyes to make a wish, but she was interrupted by Andre.

He batted his eyelashes and crooned: *Happy birthday to you, you look like dried poo, you act like a monkey and you smell like one too.*

Not to be outdone, Jardin chimed in with: *Happy birthday, happy birthday, pain and sorrow fill the air, people dying everywhere, happy birthday, happy birthday.* An eighties rock ballad, holiday cheery.

Dawn slapped her hand into Jardin's shoulder and we laughed, and then Honeyweed started singing. Her eyes twinkled, and her mouth turned up at the right corner the way that it does, and she sang quietly and sweetly: *How o-old are you, how o-old are you . . .*

Astrid closed her eyes and made her wish to a chorus of groans, and then, when Art asked, "How old are you, really?" she smiled somebody else's smile, turning the corner of her mouth up. She held her palms out and shrugged, as if she didn't know. As if years of aging didn't matter because she didn't have a much of a story either.

Astrid was a little under five-foot-six but her skinniness made her look taller somehow. She looked familiar, like someone I'd always known. The first time we met she was dressed in a sari made of warm brown cotton, and with her brown eyes and light brownish hair, I thought she looked like a leaf. A fall leaf. All silky hair and small body, unexpectedly angular at the joints. Blue green veins showed through the white skin of her hands and feet and breasts. She had one strawberry red splotch on each earlobe from a cold winter trek, a broken-down car in a blizzard maybe, or a missed bus that made her walk home from school without thinking to remove her stainless steel, cold conducting earrings . . . I never asked. She offered me her age as a gift and at her birthday I kept it to myself and she smiled.

I grumbled something to Astrid one day, as she led me through a difficult passage in his *Book of Learnings*, about Remi being oblique. She shrugged and twisted her face, as though she was above bitching behind his back, but before dinner that day, when Remi announced in his blessing that an incoming blizzard would "shake flocking peonies and repave our garden for spring," she met my eye conspiratorially.

"He's occasionally deliberate . . . " Astrid whispered, then stalled, interrupted by Jardin handing her a bowl of potatoes.

"He occasionally takes deliberate . . . " she tried again, and stopped as Remi reached in front of her for a bowl of some soupy pea green mush. I wanted the mush too.

"Please, pass the deliberate," I asked Remi.

" . . . liberties with logic," Astrid gasped in my ear.

The bastard did know what to pass me, grinned and handed me the bowl. He wasn't as wise as you'd expect the leader of a commune to be, but he had something in him. It was powerful, but also kind of annoying. He wouldn't let me leave. He told me that my life had brought me to them, and that I just needed to 'arrive'.

The brethren were gathered here, Remi claimed, so that each man among them might come to understand his place in the cosmos, how best to adapt his life to destiny. Yep, and half of them were women. Remi was giving me the opportunity to be reborn. It sounded good, if I could figure out my place in the cosmos, but I wanted to believe that the world would be waiting for me as soon as I managed to birth myself again. And I was halfway there with my name, immortal Polydeuces. Twin of Castor, half of 'the Dioscuri'.

Zeus wooed Leda as a swan so the boys were born out of eggs, Castor a mortal, Polydeuces a god. They partook of various exciting, noble, and godly exploits, and then Castor fell during a battle with his in-laws. Polydeuces was crushed. He sobbed and wailed and begged his dad to grant Castor immortality too, and finally, pestered to his limit, Zeus gave the twins joint mortality — they got to stay together, frequenting Olympus and Hades on alternate days. I don't know what Castor means in Greek, but in French it means beaver. Remi gave all of us new names and most of the brethren were stars or plants or philosophers but I was Polydeuces, P.D. And, Remi assured that, so named, I was 'welcome among them'. Among us.

At my naming in the fall, everybody had been meant to be dancing a dream, instead of waiting to dream one. There were drums and music on CD and their contortions should have been corny but were kind of beautiful. I had trouble picturing the ritual catching on in wider society the way Remi wanted it to, but the dance, or perhaps the drugs, brought tears to my eyes. The fluttery music brought phrases like 'hither and yon' into my head and I felt ready. I wanted that sky dwelling timeless youth crap Remi rambled on about. They wrapped me up in brown canvas and I squiggled my way out, a larval butterfly embracing its laborious ecdysis from cocoon and caterpillar skin.

Post-celebration, we newly hatched butterflies were hungover, breakfast was late, and everyone took longer-than-usual showers. I got the last draw as the latest arrival and ran out of hot water. I ended up bathing in a stream of ice that could barely dissolve the homemade sage-scented soap. I was trying to rub soap scum off with a towel, ripping scabs from skinned knees in the process, when Remi poked his head into the bathroom and asked for confirmation that I'd seen something I wanted to become a part of. I scrubbed the towel across my face and gave Remi what seemed like the simplest answer, "Yeah."

He eased me in with a series of enigmatic notes:

Wisdom is an architect

We cast our own shadows

The whole of the truth is shown once it is plucked free

He usually winked when he gave them to me. To be friendly, I guess. But the more time I spent with Remi, the less I liked him. I can't really explain why, except that, clearly, confusing notes are the last thing a confused man wants to read. Also, he smiled like he knew things about you that you didn't know about yourself, and it seemed entirely possibly that this was true. His voice was disarming, in a way that made me guiltily suspicious of it. With his soft consonants, it was the voice of European politicians and telemarketing investment bankers and late-evening college radio hosts. A voice designed to make you drop your guard and open your wallet and/or impressionable brain. His breath smelled like fennel, and he was touchy in a less than paternal way. He ran his index finger along the women's jaw lines and down their spines in answer to the least sexual inquiries. He walked his index and middle finger down my arm while he explained things to me. I suspect these were distraction tactics. His notes were kind of cool but he couldn't always explain them, and he never answered questions quite head on. For example, who was I?

"A blank slate," he said, frowning.

I tried to engage. I completed my readings, discussed them with Art and Astrid, and sat in silence two hours each day. I felt healthier, but I still didn't know who I was. Or what I was called to do in the community. When Winter Solstice failed to prompt true transformation Remi arranged a sweat lodge ritual for Groundhog Day. It was supposed to purify me, and I suppose it did. I was looking, and then I was found. In a cold, solid place. The land where things are too real.

Within the darkened dome Remi whispered that water, "is the lifeblood." He poured a ladle of water over heated stones, sending up a cloud of steam to scorch our throats.

"Earth," Art shouted, "holds the soul, the tomb, and the sustenance of man." Something light and peppery landed across my chest, earth and ash.

"Air," Astrid's voice stumbled over her words. *"Air!"* she shouted, at a loss, and shoved the flap door open to let in a gust of cold winter air. I felt Andre's lungs expand against my side as we gasped that freshness in.

"Fire," Jardin whispered, and clicked a flame to life, a lighter held at chest level. He looked around at us, and we looked at ourselves, suddenly revealed. We were sweaty and seated awkwardly on our heels or thighs to minimize the discomfort of the needles and branches we'd spread to mat the floor. Astrid's long hair hung limply across her shoulders and breasts, Andre's was spiked where he'd run his hands through it, and Remi's curls were plastered damply to his forehead. Kate kneeled with her head down near the coolness of the floor, and two wrinkly breasts swung against the curve of her belly as she shifted her weight to her elbows and looked up.

"Fire," Jardin said again, clicking us back into darkness, "reveals and conceals, destroys and births, ends and begins."

And something moved through our circle then. Something like a wind, or a push, the oscillation of a spring. A chain of spiritual yawns that rippled through us around the lodge. Something real. I felt so tied to the people around me that I barely noticed when they began to move. I acknowledged the sound of shifting bodies absently, they were like a shifting handful of my own thoughts — but then a draft of air moved between Andre and me as he turned towards Remi on his left, and a clutch of fingers slipped into the bend of my folded knee. I don't know whose fingers they were.

Jardin was on the other side of the stones, so they probably belonged to Kate, or maybe Honeyweed. I shuddered. I had sat down in the wrong part of the circle. I was diving back to individuality and the individual me didn't want to be there. I might have vomited if there had anything in my stomach to vomit but we'd fasted. I tried to stand and crashed into the arc of a sapling, scratching my neck and shoulder. There were four hands on my thighs when I dove for the door.

With hindsight, maybe those hands reached out of concern. I don't really think that they would have forced me to do anything — they would have guided me to the door if I'd asked for it. They were 'sounding' their bodies with touch. But when I crashed through the doorflap the cold air slapped me to the ground and I clung to it, frightened by the intensity of my relief. When I raised my head, I saw Astrid beside me, shivering and concerned, all parts pert in the cold.

"Too much?" she asked.

I tried to lower my face but she lifted my head.

I wished it was day, afternoon, and that all I had to do was stand in the kitchen and wash something. I had sex with Astrid instead. With muffled prayers coming from inside the lodge for mood music, Astrid and I melted a human-shaped hole in the snow. She was on top and I looked up at her and at the stars past her and beside us there were stones squalling and splitting, spitting their heat.

Remi left the door to his office open most of the time and the phone sat on his desk, so I could have called the police or something. I even picked up the handset one day, but that was mid-February. They needed me to make the craft quota and I suppose it felt important to be needed. It was easy to do nothing. The thought of leaving made me as ill as staying and as the days got longer and brighter I told Astrid the sun was rising and setting farther and farther north. Closer and closer to us.

"I think a woman should be however she wants to be," I said.

I picked a piece of bark from a log and dropped it into fresh snow. It had fallen almost constantly since the sweat lodge ceremony and the hole we'd melted was gone. The chips left pockmarks in a deep bank that had blown up against the woodpile.

"However she *is*," Astrid stressed.

I nodded. I loved sitting there with her in the night with the wind in the trees muttering above us. I nodded to keep her talking and kept my eyes on her bony fingers, fluttering in the moonlight. Her hair, slipping out from her woolly toque. I wanted to say something nice.

"The real problem," she insisted, breathy and excited by her thoughts, "is that men don't see women as part of themselves."

"No, they don't." I tried, "I mean, I guess so, you know . . . "

"You guys see us as *other*."

I shook my head in denial.

"You do," she smiled. "We give birth to you, and take care of you, and mature faster and humour your ways."

She was looking past me to the light above the kitchen door. "The sexes blind people to our *united* humanity."

I frowned and loved her.

"I think," she squinted at the dark, "I think that sometimes if a woman has a good idea, a man won't agree with it or support it, even though if it were thought up by a man, he might agree with it."

"Did you think of something?" I asked.

She smiled, "No. No, but I think that a lot of guys ignore female intelligence."

I waited.

"It's too much for them for woman to be sexy and smart at once." She shook her head, "It's too much power."

I punched my mittened fist gently at the air between us, "Power."

She smiled, but she looked really sad. Someone was not listening to Astrid's good ideas. I reached for her hand. I listened, nodded, and commiserated through the quietest part of the night, and by the time I crawled into my bunk bed she'd said that we mustn't fall in love.

I dreamt that night that I was holding a woman. She slept in my arms, her head resting heavy on my shoulder. Her lips were soft against each other, her own ear curled around itself, but I got to hold her. Her hair was smooth against my face but when I tried to kiss her, in the magic way that dreams move, our positions changed so that I was in her arms suddenly and she was shaking me. Slapping me, crying, and shouting my real name.

By March it was clear that Astrid had come to loggerheads with Remi over something she didn't want to tell me about. Vespers became increasingly dramatic.

"If pity and compassion and tenderness visit her heart, if she leave my work to toy with old sweetnesses, then shall my vengeance be known!" Remi thundered. Andre whispered 'The Book of the Law,' in my ear. So Remi's recitations were from Crowley, the words narrated in the crypt of a pyramid by a praeterhuman intelligence at noon on April 8, 9, and 10, 1904. It was all part of the assigned reading, but I didn't recognize the words coming out of his mouth. Remi was grinning as if he had just made us from clay and was about to show us off to his friends. Kate rose to sashay around the room, painted toes glinting in the firelight, a red tasselled mini-dress swinging around her thighs. "Every number is infinite: there is no difference!"

I tried Art first, because he seemed the most intellectual about things. The least likely, I thought, to feel hurt.

I said, "I was wondering how I might — not that I am thinking of it, really — I'm just curious, hypothetically, how' I'd go about . . . "

He interrupted me with a sigh. "You want to know how to leave?"

I nodded. He sighed again, and reminded me that I still didn't know why I'd come to Hadit's Wood in the first place.

"The outsiders would drain you," he reminded me gently. "If people were concerned for your safety and looking for you, they would have found you by now. It wouldn't be that hard to track you down. Hadit's Wood is a listed commune on federal registries. Besides," he added, "if no one is looking for you, you may not have been a man that others cared to love. Now," he smiled, "now, you have a whole community that loves you too much to lose you, and you have a whole community of people to love."

Art mostly wanted to quell dissent, I guess. He knew I cared about Astrid and also Andre. I did care about Andre. In a protective, dissociated sense. He was like a little brother to me, and I might have talked about leaving with him, except he was out on a vision quest in the melting woods. Astrid had taught me new words to mean love, but I suspected she was ready to shake me free.

I followed Astrid's path across the yard one day, intending to waylay her on her way back from the craft Quonset, but turned at the sound of the Land Rover. Remi was returning from a trip somewhere and Kate was gazing dejectedly out of the passenger side window. Remi turned to her and said something to make her pout, then ruffled his palm over her hair and pushed her out of the car to open the door to the barn. As they pulled in I saw something more interesting. Another car. Parked inside the barn, between bales of hay and canisters of honey and goat feed, I could see wheels poking out from beneath a green tarp.

There were only four buildings at Hadit's Wood, but apparently I had never thoroughly investigated the barn. I'd been in there for introductions to the baby goats, but didn't linger. I was kind of weirded out by Kate, Remi's sister, who tended the animals and machinery. As she and Remi made for the main building with boxes of dry goods and a fat coil of rainbow hemp, I slipped into the shadowy barn and lifted the edge of the tarp.

It was dark and hard to see after the bright morning sun outside. It smelled of mildew and goat. I squeezed between a bale and the car's drivers side door and, finding it unlocked, slid under the tarp and into the driver's seat. It was a space as still and hollow as a snail's shell. Dark as anything. I ran my hands over the steering wheel and jumped at a sound beneath me. Probably just a kitten or a mouse, or a kitten and a mouse. Nothing to panic about. I reached for the interior light switch and it came on, so the battery was charged. It illuminated blue plastic molding and black and orange dials. I closed my hands around the steering wheel and it felt as familiar as zipping up an old pair of jeans. I cried in the driver's seat until my stomach started to growl and I heard the chimes that signaled suppertime. Even then, I waited awhile, wiping my face with my shirt. I had to look like I'd just been visiting the barn, like I was just returning from an innocent goat-visiting trip to the barn.

In the dining room, I took my seat quietly and thanked Astrid when she passed me a basket of sliced bread, and Kate, who ladled some chunky green soup into my bowl.

I thought of the car, of driving away. P.D. who? I was Dustin McKeowan and the soup was mealy. I wanted a drive-thru. My spoon rattled on the edge of my bowl. I scooped up a spoonful and let it fall back in with a splat and no one said a thing.

I had to talk to someone, but was suspicious of Remi and Art, didn't like Kate or Jardin, barely ever talked to Alberta and Delia, didn't trust Honeyweed not to run to Remi, and couldn't very well tell Dawn without telling Don. I volunteered to check on Andre that night, but Jardin had already signed on for the task. That left Astrid, sitting to my left, who drew her finger down the back of my neck and invited me to read her new journal entry. I smiled a shaky response over a saucer of the expired tinned peaches Dawn served for dessert.

Being a worried and slightly nauseous Dustin J. McKeowan was not nearly as exciting as being the mysteriously mortal twin to a Greek beaver. I wondered if Astrid would still love me. I imagined her saying something like, no, she didn't love me, she loved man, of which I was a part.

"What do you mean, realized something?" Is what she actually said. I'd been vague, testing the waters in the privacy of her bedroom after dutifully scanning her journal entry. I'd said nothing about the car in the barn.

"Well . . . I, um," I had to stop procrastinating, "You call me P.D. — My name is Dustin, I'm from Edmonton..."

Astrid evaluated me carefully, running her eyes over my chest and hands. She shook her head a couple of times, as if she was about to speak, but kept quiet for the longest two minutes ever.

"My name is Tiffany," she said, and then she picked my hands up with her own and placed them on her hips, but it wasn't the same as before.

Traplines

The sky was filled with Vs of geese that whole week. It was April already, and they were returning north. I don't know how long it's been since the Canada Goose evolved itself into existence, but watching them fly over, I imagined millennia of geese honking their way north and south and north again. Andre told me a joke about geese before he went questing.

"Yo, P.D., why is one side of a V of geese always longer than the other side?"

"Because geese stagger their flight to maximize their aerodynamics . . . "

"P.D. — This is a joke."

I tilted my head back, slid my eyes after the flying geese, Vs offset and overlapping like fish scales in the sky. I gave up. "Why?"

"'Cause there's more geese in it."

Andre's jokes usually involved whores, lepers, or preists, but his ears blushed when he laughed about Vs of geese. I pushed him into a bush. He pushed me back. I missed that, and looked up for geese again. Off above the woods they made low and dull sounds that seemed to echo. Maybe it was geese answering each other, talking back and forth under the heavy sky.

Astrid was distracted over breakfast, spilled supplies and fumbled with glue in the craft room, and wasn't hungry at lunch. I watched her staring at Kate staring at her bowl. The mushroom soup tasted like dirt. Pepper didn't help. I caught up to Astrid between the house and the Quonset after lunch and asked her to leave with me.

"How?" she asked.

I told her about the second car in the shed, the unlabelled car key I'd seen hanging from a tack in Remi's office, the live battery, and the empty tank of gas. She grabbed the waist of my pants and pulled me through the door of the Quonset.

I expected a grateful embrace. Maybe more, though I'd been cut off for a few weeks. She pushed me into a chair by the side of the stove and told me a story about a cat that ran away. Her family moved but six years later it found them. It showed up at their doorstep, even though they had moved to a new province. It was exactly the same cat, with the same patch of frostbitten fur on its ear and the same red and green plaid collar. Its name was Jenny.

"Okay," I said.

"We were so happy to see her," Astrid explained, tears in her eyes.

I would have been charmed a month earlier, when afternoon meant almost evening, and evening meant mugs up. I was still kind of charmed, but it was April and midday the sky was the whitest possible shade of grey.

"Do you want to leave?" I asked. "Do you want me to get the key?"

She looked hurt, worried, and possibly angry. She nodded.

We didn't plot our escape in the Land Rover because, firstly, its absence would be noticed much more quickly than that of the ancient Ford Escort; and second, they might, I imagined, be more likely to charge us with theft. I wanted to divorce Hadit's Wood legally, but we didn't want to tell people that we were leaving because Astrid was pretty sure that they'd try to stop us. Remi would give long, guilt-inspiring lectures and Art would remind us how happy we'd been and how dangerous it was in the world at large. Apparently, that woman Helen's announcement that she wanted to leave was followed by months of guilt-tripping and attempted brainwashing. Eventually she 'left in the night', without proper goodbyes. Indeed. Had anyone else seen the bones in the compost?

I stole the non-Land Rover key from the bulletin board in Remi's office during the excitement of Andre's return from his quest. He spent the afternoon locked in his room with Remi, relating his vision and preparing himself to preach a sermon after dinner. Everyone was giddy and Astrid and I tried our best to fit in. We brewed cider in the kitchen and took turns nipping back and forth to our rooms to pack our things. Well, her things. I had a journal, jacket, and toothbrush.

We met in the barn at four o'clock. I arrived first, startling the goat and its bell rang out around the yard. Astrid followed, darting through beams of sunlight with our supplies bundled in her arms. But that night, she left without me. And it was too dark (or I was too drunk) to find a way to follow her. Salt in a paper cut, Jesus and Joseph, Art would have said. And shit on a stick. I was too tired to be angry, too lonely to let myself cry. Astrid left and I tried to follow on foot, finally sinking down at the base of a tree, a desperate waiting place for light and morning. Half of me wanted to crawl back to my bunk, but there lay Remi, the brush of his stubble, his questions, his expectant eyes. In the woods, whose shadows I could barely squint through, there was a space apart from that. A room for the Dustin who might be me to sleep and dream.

I woke in dissolving dark to Remi cursing in Hadit's name and someone (I bet on Art) kicking the Land Rover's tires. I stood and bounced to get my blood moving. It was incredible to think that Andre had stayed out for four days and three nights. He'd at least had a sleeping bag. I had only a thin jacket. A door slammed shut, bounced open, and was pulled firmly closed off to my right. I walked in the opposite direction until all human sounds were crowded out of my ears by crackling branches and the squish of my feet against frosty moss. I wanted solitude and to get away. A half-dreamt plan involved following the stream that drained the pond to a bigger stream, which would connect to an even bigger stream, which would eventually lead me to civilization. It seemed a foolproof escape, until I saw the beaver. Snared and stiff, glittering with beaded dew.

It had been chewing through the rubber hosing of the intake line from the water pump. I know Jardin had caught and relocated it a few times before we voted to kill it. The holes it made in the line sucked in algae that clogged up the hot water tank and it had come down to a choice between the beaver or warm showers. The beaver's stubbornness saved me — in the pragmatic, rather than metaphorical sense. If Jardin hadn't been checking the trap they might not have found me for days. I mean, really, could I have followed a stream a hundred and fifty kilometres without food? I would have been ripped apart by animals. Bitten by bush fever. I'm not Davy Crockett or Paul Bunyan or whatever. That beaver's teeth were streaked yellow and orange and I hadn't expected that, but of course wild animals don't brush.

As far as I know, Castor is languishing in the ice pit, waiting for someone to get brave enough to eat meat. We don't like to waste around here. I am working at not being wasteful with Astrid's loss. I am building myself in the absence of her definition. I like to picture the beaver returned to the woods, tireless, methodical — he is chewing down trees, nibbling their leaves, dragging their branches and trunks into place. Industrious as only a beaver can be, he paces himself. He has all the time in the world to plan the spreading of the creek into a well-treed pond. A wind-sheltered mirror where, at dawn, the reflection of his lodge in the water will make a perfect 'O'.

The Jasmine Springs Road

TIM EXPECTED THE TRAIN TO CLIMB into the mountains but it rocked along beneath them, tracking the edges of valleys flatter and wider than he'd ever seen before. There were grassy and shrubby stretches, but flashing past the windows, most of what they saw were trees. Aspen, poplar and dogwood trembling beside the track, White and Engleman Spruce marching up the slopes towards sharp bare peaks. Tim's father, Bo, named the trees for him. From the seat ahead, Flint muttered that he didn't know these woods from 'wally' — but he was the one, once they'd set into cutting the road, who flagged and felled them. Tim loved trees, but fell deeper in love that summer with saw oil, and the green cut, and earth tearing open when their roots came up.

Nobody knew who found the springs, but coal miners built the first pool. Black dust floated up off their bodies and marked lines around the rocks they'd stacked. Yellow sulphur frothed out of the water where it spilled over the lip of their pool, and floated back at them in sudsy clumps. It stank, for sure, but no worse than a coal seam, and the miners came out of their black-marked baths whiter than most of them could remember being. Clean white like a plate the queen could eat off of. Snow white like they'd got better jobs than they did.

Bo told Tim this story three days into grading the road cut. He meant, wash your face, Tiam li, and when Tim resisted, Bo pushed him into a bucket of night-chilled water set out beside their tent.

Jiam bo had been with the rail crew that blew the aquifers open back in the twenties. He knew the valley, and he knew grading, but he still felt eyes on him when he they hired him on to the road crew. There'd been talk of laws, work for whites first. And then he'd had to drag a kid along, eating free. If he kept his son clean, quiet, and willing, nobody seemed to mind. Not halfway up a mountain. They tipped mints into Tim's pockets and fed him swears and stories that he shoved in his boots, safekept.

"Is he apt to be useful?" Flint asked, when Bo, set to blasting stumps, tried to shake Tim off.

Flint came from Australia where there's nothing but wild dogs to eat you. Tim was born in Vancouver and saw a grizzly bear only once before Bo took him into the mountains. It was a brown, wet-looking lump eating thrown-out fish at the nuisance grounds — nothing to be scared of — so Flint pointed out different ways Tim could scramble down to the stream for water. He lifted Tim's hat off his shoulders and patted it down on his head, winking, "It's only mehd dogs and Englishmen what run abeet in mid-die sun."

After the first few trips, sliding and stumbling, practising new swears, Tim's job paced itself. On the way down, he massaged his hands, running scabs over the smooth softness that stayed, untouched, in the centre of his palms. Between Bo's blasting, the crack of trees, and the truck coming up and down, there was a lot of noise. Still, Tim hallooed and crashed, bold and fast, every time he approached the stream and the salmonberry bushes beside it. The water barrel bounced between his shoulder blades, and his heart would race a mile a minute, but there was never anything but sheep, elk, and marmots. And big, bold crows.

The Jasmine Springs Road

On the way up Tim had to move slowly, grabbing at trees for balance at steep parts. The water barrel sloshed between his shoulders, pulling and shifting its weight. It was a living thing that he continued to feel moving against his back after he'd set it down. It became an effort, that summer, to stop moving. In the evenings the men gathered for news, schedules, and talking. Dinner plate scraped, mug drained, Tim clamped his feet to the ground, trying to belong.

"Runny blood sickness," Bo said.

If that girl ever got cut she could never stop bleeding. Tim had a hanky wrapped around a cut on his knuckle and Bo pointed to it, turning every whisky-slack face onto his son's effort to be still.

Bo said that Little Jasmine's father had read about water curing people in the Bible. Then he read about springs curing people in the newspaper. Then he wrapped his little girl up in a quilt, let her mother kiss her, and climbed onto a train. It was a long ride to the mountains, and the trip seemed even longer when they got out at an empty station. Remember, Bo said, the mine closed down before the war opened it up again. When Little Jasmine and her father got off the train, that station was pretty well dead. The only person there was an old Indian lady standing with a horse. She said, "Hey, you, give me that girl and I'll take her for a bath."

Little Jasmine's father didn't trust this old lady one bit. Her breath smelled, her body smelled, and she looked funny at his daughter.

He said, "Five dollars for your horse."

"No," She said, "You give me that girl and I'll take her for a good bath."

"Ten dollars," the father said, "fifteen." That lady didn't say a thing, so he just pushed money at her and put Little Jasmine on the horse and led it away. They went to the end of the emptied out

mine shacks and they followed a rough sign that pointed up a path to Miner's Springs.

"Don't worry, Little Jasmine," her father said, "we'll have you cured tomorrow." He believed it, too. He made a camp at the side of the path for them to sleep one night in the woods and in the morning he thought they would see the valley where the springs were. The newspaper said you could see steam rising up, a signpost in the trees. Come morning there was a fog so thick all around them that they couldn't see more than a few feet anywhere. They could barely see each other. The father found the horse by listening hard for its breathing. When he reached out and caught its halter something red moved fast in the fog beside him but it was gone when he turned to look.

"Did you see something, Little Jasmine?" he asked.

"Yes," she said, "the lady was pointing to the spring. That way, by the stream."

"No," her father said, "the spring is on the east side of this valley." It said so in the newspaper, and he unfolded it from his pocket and showed her.

They sat together and looked west into the fog where Little Jasmine thought she'd seen someone until the girl whispered, "She looked like she was in a hurry."

"We'll wait for this fog to clear up," her father replied, but he couldn't wait easy. He wrapped Little Jasmine up in her quilt and lifted her onto the horse, to keep her warm and ready to go. He stood by the horse's head, holding it steady. Twice he thought he saw something red move in the whiteness. Maybe a fox, but it never came close enough to tell. The third time, he smelled something too. Rotten egg smell. The horse shivered. The father felt wind pushing up his hat. That wind got stronger and colder and then, finally, blew off the fog except for one twist of white in the trees ahead of them — the springs, not so far away, and on the west side of the valley, wouldn't you know. But when Little Jasmine's father stepped the horse forward it jumped at something under the bushes and Little Jasmine slipped off.

The quilt made for a soft fall, but it didn't keep a scraggly branch from scratching Little Jasmine's face on her way from the horse to the ground. Two long red lines, one on Little Jasmine's forehead, one on her soft-as-silk cheek.

They'd got so close to the spring that all Little Jasmine's father could think was, you couldn't have done this falling back home? He kissed his daughter, five, ten, fifteen times, but that runny blood kept draining out of her. Her yellow dress turned red and her face drained white as a plate the queen would eat off of. Little Jasmine's father smelled something sweet and looked up and finally caught a good look at the fox that had been circling around them in the fog. Red and scruffy, quick on black feet. When he looked down again his Little Jasmine was still as a doll, floppy and wet from the fog and her own useless blood.

Her father wrapped the quilt around Little Jasmine's tiny dead body and carried her to the stream she'd pointed to. He laid her down beside it and covered her over with rocks. He spent one night lying on the ground beside Little Jasmine and then, cold to the inside of his bones, he went looking for the horse in the trees.

The horse whinnied and tripped and pulled back against Little Jasmine's father the whole way down the mountain. Maybe it was nervous because Little Jasmine's father was smelling like blood and death. Maybe it didn't like the sound of coins, ringing together in a pocket. Little Jasmine's father heard that sound too, but every time he turned around, all he saw was the horse, nobody else.

The Indian lady was waiting at the empty train station. She said, no, she couldn't buy that horse back, she spent all that money already. She got the horse anyway, though, because Little Jasmine's father couldn't afford to put it on the train. She got to keep Little

Jasmine too. And that girl looks perfect now, all cleaned up except for those two cuts on her white as a moon face. Maybe she smells a bit like rotting meat and an old woman's body, but Bo said that when she gets close enough to people that little ghost still asks if they'll take her home.

Washing his dishes under the cook's lantern, Tim saw moths circle in on the reflection of the flame on the water. They floated, kicking. Lifted out, they smeared apart, leaving dark smudges on the wooden stand.

Tim worried that the road, as it progressed, would disturb Little Jasmine's bones — it followed the stream's valley and ran parallel to it in sections.

"Is no father, no girl," Jiam bo asserted.

But what if Little Jasmine started following Tim because he was closest to her age? Or because of the cut on his knuckle that kept opening up to bleed again. Or because, out of the whole crew, he was the only one who again and again had to slide down to rocks at the edge of the stream. What if he landed on her?

"Is story, Tiam li. There's enough."

Bo meant, get undressed, go to sleep. Tim could hear moths outside, thwacking against lantern glass and he felt his cot rock with a barrel's weight of water. When Bo had told the part about Little Jasmine falling off the horse, he'd used Tim's face to show the cuts. He'd pulled his son into the lantern light and jabbed a finger at Tim's face, smearing dirty lines to show the rivers of Little Jasmine's blood. As he fell asleep, Tim felt those lines, the drawn movement of them, returning.

By late July they could see the twists of steam rising up from the valley ahead of them. When he caught whiffs of sulfur on the wind, Tim scanned the trees, looking for foxes and keeping track of where Bo and Flint were working. He was disappointed, his first trip up, to find out that the springs were just big wooden bathtubs.

The road crew added a canvas dressing room to the cluster of tents pitched in the rubble beside the springs. Evenings and afternoons off they soaked in drawers and undershirts and counted their baths as laundry. Bo said the water was too hot for bones that were growing, or in his own case, bones that were old. So Tim washed their laundry in the stream on Sundays, but still went up to perch on the edge of the tubs at night. Off the hook to entertain, Bo suddenly didn't seem to mind being left alone. The lanterns had tattooed Bo's face with shadows at their old camp, making his accent mysterious and authentic Tim had thought. Now the lanterns swung over the tubs after wash up. The surface of the water rippled up when Tim lowered his feet in it, spreading shadows like lines and blobs of ink.

Sometimes mats of algae came loose from the rocks at the spring vents and floated down in oily black rafts that turned snot coloured in daylight. Those mats were firm and slippery as fish. Flint scooped them out of the water with his hands, but they sent shivers up Tim's back. He felt the same thing when his feet, dangling into the water, rubbed against the slimy side of the boards. Flint slid his whole hairy red body down those boards and sighed, "Ah, Mate."

Flint thought Bo was missing out, shy of something. It was true that Bo had scars on his shoulders he didn't like showing. Long ropy ones that Flint didn't know were there. It was Flint, not Bo, who let on to Tim how the springs got named.

The railway tried to clear grade right though them. They blasted into the rock beside the spring and the smell cracked from high rotten egg to nothing. The blasting boss told Flint that half his crew was knocked out, but they did all come around, some quicker and with less slapping or shaking than others. A curious thing was that the last ones waking up remembered something sweet coming out of the rocks and dust.

"New snow no smell!" one of them shouted, stumbling up — then "Jasmine smell!"

"Can ye guess who that'd be, Teem?"

A smell like green jasmine tea, sharp, floral, barely there. Miner's Springs got renamed Jasmine Springs because the mapping engineer marked what the Jiam bo, the Chinaman, said best.

The sulphur gas coming up with the spring water was harmless until it got heavy, Flint explained. Then, denser than air, it could push the oxygen out of your lungs. Same as sour gas in a coal seam, the air over the springs could turn poisonous if the wind was weak or if a jolt like the blast released what was pent up underground. Early on, one of the road workers leaned a board up beside the pools that said: SMELL MATCHES? A.O.K. SMELL NOTHING? R.U.N.

The newspaper said, *With strong physiologic effect, Canada's Rocky Mountain springs are world-class destinations for travellers seeking the miracles of hydrotherapy.*

Sulfur steamed up in more than one place in the valley around Jasmine's Springs and might've eaten through track, so the railway laid the freight line a valley over. It wasn't until the thirties that a road to Jasmine's Springs started making as much sense as the other projects Ottawa was dreaming up as a way to make jobs. A make-work project, and plenty enough sick and unemployed to benefit.

Once they'd set up camp at the springs, with the stream right beside them, Tim's barrel got hauled by whoever needed water right then. They set him instead to picking too-big rocks out of the lower road, where the gravel was planed. Busywork because he was really on standby to take deliveries and intercept sick people trying to come up.

"Good afternoon, sorry, but the road's not done, the rest of the way is still rough so you might want to turn around."

If they were too sick they turned around, but a lot charged through, stalling work. Some arthritic ladies came up on donkeys and they were the first who said they'd seen her. Halfway up the valley to Jasmine's Springs they saw this pale little girl in a red and brown dress who tried to hide when they called out to her. She slipped away, moving in and out of the trees.

"That'll be Little Jasmine," one of the men reassured, when they came down insisting someone go and find her. "She stays out of the way, most of the time."

There was a doctor who hiked up the road and he looked perfectly healthy but shook his head, nope. He said he had rotten luck, short days, so Tim walked with him for a ways, warning him about the road being rough farther up, and the sulphur gas. How if he did smell anything more than the struck matches smell he should be very careful. Also that he should watch for any strange animals or girls who smelled bad. Though he shouldn't worry too much about animals because there were lots of real ones around the springs too, and some were musky ones.

"Often sheep, and deer, but also a lot of bears, even cougars. Also there's a ghost'"

The doctor nodded skeptically and said that he'd heard.

"It's maybe just stories," Tim admitted.

"Yes and no," the doctor said, "Runny blood sickness is a simple way to say haemophilia." A very real disease. And a real person who had that disease was a prince, the doctor said, and small cuts were much less of a problem for him than bruises. A bruise is bleeding inside your skin and hot water would only make that bleeding worse.

Mid-August Flint had said no one could tell Chinese age and turned Tim fourteen and old enough to be paid half wages. This way Tim and Bo would get two cheques at the end of the summer, their pay less expenses. The end of that summer had seemed far away at first, but the black of the trees ate up all kinds of sparks that Tim wished, halfway, would catch and carry.

One night at the tubs Flint poured whisky into a jar of spring water to show Tim how alcohol doesn't mix right with sulfur water. A yellow film of sulfur formed over the top of the jar. Inside, the two liquids swirled apart, spring water sinking and alcohol rising up. This was kind of hard to see, both liquids being pretty well clear. Flint called it separating, but the swirling apart looked like spirits twisting under water. The yellow skin might be what was holding those immiscibles in.

"No ghost spirits," Bo said in their tent. And later, "Waste of whisky."

White men always waste whisky, Bo said. One time there was a man who found a bear who knew how to play baseball and drink whisky. Then it stopped playing baseball and all it wanted to do was drink whisky. That was okay at first, though, because lots of people wanted to watch that bear get drunk. But one night, it got really drunk and then it chewed through its rope and ran away with that man's wallet. All his money.

"You understand, Tiam li?"

Tim nodded. But he didn't understand, exactly. That bear was a man who got turned into a bear, he guessed, but was he white or was the man who found him white?

"Is story, Tiam li," Bo sighed.

Tim finished for him, "No bear, no whisky." And Jiam bo laughed. Tim laughed too, tasting blood in his mouth. It was a stupid story but he had bitten the inside of his cheeks, trying to listen properly.

Near the end, when they dragged the road right up to the spring and were levelling ground for a proper pool, that was when Tim started wondering. Was it Little Jasmine's father's fault that she died? Or was it the Indian lady's? What would have happened if they had taken Little Jasmine for that bath, considering how hot water made haemophilia worse? Was it the fox's fault Little Jasmine died or was he trying to keep her safe?

Tim washed his fork and plate, kicked his tar-patched boots together and considered the fact that, in two months, he had yet to see a fox, or an Indian for that matter. Is story, Tiam li, Bo would say. No father, no girl. And if he'd asked for new boots (which some of the men had ordered up) it would've been, no money. Never mind that he was making his own money. And there was too a girl Tim knew by then. He had heard a lot of people telling about her, even if Bo only smelled the Jasmine smell because, being the Chinaman, he was closest to the blast in the first place, and the last guy anybody remembered to slap awake.

Late September, a half-retained crew built a conservation cabin up by the spring, all walls and no roof. The roof would be tin, brought up the next spring. A carpenter, Jossy, came and bossed them to strip and fit logs so they'd lock watertight when they swelled into each other. He said the building would last, jointed and fitted, as long as anything could that close to steam. Ottawa had shipped up a crate of nails, though, so the night before the inspectors drove up, Flint and Bo pounded them in through solid fitted joints for good and useless measure.

When he found out, Jossy swore the nails would rust out in a day and that the building was a recipe for black liquor. Not something to drink, but a sludge that comes out of wood decayed too fast. A kind of alcohol that's meant for burning, Jossy said, which is what God made alcohol for.

Flint and Bo had stayed up late, hammering all those nails. Tim had watched, outside the pool of lamplight. They were drinking and it made Flint's face soft and happy and Bo's eyes red. Bo forgot to have a proper accent and rambled on in English that sounded like he didn't know any better. He mumbled on about Tim's mom, scalding her hands at the Vancouver General hospital laundry. He'd sent her back the next day. Bo dropped a lot of nails, bars that glinted up the next morning from the gravel around the cabin's base.

They were packing out on a Monday. On the last Friday he had, Tim peeled out of his clothes and sank his body down into the hottest pool, the one closest to the springs. He gasped at the pull of the heat on his muscles, at the grip of it around his groin. He felt needles pushing in and out of his feet where they touched down on the slimy rocks at the bottom. He had sneaked away from dinner, timing his immersion so that no one from the crew would be there who could laugh, or tell. Once he adjusted to the heat, Tim halfway wished someone were there. To see that he was in up to his neck, swirling the stinking foam through the water with his hands. It was a secret Bo would have to guess, by the smell of it on Tim's skin. By the match strike that would follow his son's body into their tent.

Sunday, Tim walked away from the tents and found Bo standing on a raised concrete trough they'd poured to drain water from the new pools to the stream. He turned his head at Tim's footsteps, lifting two fingers to cover his lips. He waved for Tim to climb up beside him. There were elk over the lip of the trough.

Two females, heads lowered to lick the rocks where spring water splashed down to the stream bank.

Elk were everywhere that summer and Tim cleared his throat to say so, but stopped when the animals' heads rose. Their noses, puffing warm, visible breath, came almost even with Tim's feet. He had the sudden, impossible idea that his father wanted to leap off the trough and ride away on one of these creatures' backs. Bo's body tilted forwards and moved against Tim's arm and the bag Flint had handed him to deliver. Tim was not supposed to know (but it was impossible that he wouldn't know) that the bag held a bottle of whisky bought out of their pay. Two dollars that would be gone before they were packed. Less rent for the winter, more work for his mother. Tim shifted the bag, crinkling it so his father would notice, but Jiam bo was still looking down.

At their feet the elk were big but calm and quiet. These were not like Tim's bears. He had seen elk often in daylight, stepping clumsily around the boulders at the edge of the stream. Now they seemed to be watching him and his father, moist eyes still, noses shivering. The elk were wondering, maybe, if Bo and Tim were real. Human beings were the novelties at Jasmine's Springs. Elk knew about the sulfur and the warmth of the water before the road came in, before the rail crew, before the coal miners or the Indians. Before time came along, or stories.

"There your ghosts, Tiam li," Bo said, when the elk finally turned.

Round white faces bobbed and slipped into the trees across. Elk bums by moonlight, Tim knew. A girl and an Indian, bowing and backing away.

Tango Medio

SO THERE'S THIS BOOK THAT SAYS that the key to good sex is a thirteen-letter word, not sado-masochism, nope. Communication. Bees speak through their bodies. They dance, wiggle and spin, buzz angled zigs and zags. They smell each other, wafting odour-rich plumes that yield the directions and distance to pollen. They are a sorority of women who feed each other, chewing and spitting into each other's mouths. They flavour their saliva with outdoor temperature, humidity, and the progress of their queen's march towards menopause. Do they hold the last back, regurgitating for the drones? The furry males they coddle through summer, fatten, and kick, spent, into autumn frost. They don't need to know what's coming. These patterns, this waxed geometry, it all happens without the bees appearing to think.

I decided I had to break up with Darryl when sex started to remind me of baking. The kind you eat to be polite. I've had a lot of experience with sub-par baking, thanks to his mom. His dad's a beekeeper and his mom, convinced that artificially refined sugar contains more calories, substitutes honey in all of her recipes. It doesn't taste that bad, but it all tastes like honey, too rich to eat in volume. After you've had one kind of cookie, you've kind of had them all. I couldn't imagine committing to waking up to the same taste, monotonous monochrism, every morning for the rest of my life.

At night, Darryl is too tired, worked out already by the bees. He's tired on market days too, after dealing with Hutterites. They sell at the Farmer's Market Saturdays, and out of Darryl's dad's garage on Tuesdays. I go after classes on Tuesdays to help. They sell by weight and people conveniently forget to weigh their buckets before filling them, so we courteously subtract a 'grace' amount. It's on the heavy side, generously estimating the bucket's weight. I did some mass balances one day and figure they're cheated out of ten to fifteen pounds of honey a month. There are regular non-Hutterite clients too but Darryl is convinced it's the Hutterites dodging the tare. They buy from us when their yields are low, which is getting to be pretty often since they won't use antifungals. They don't use zippers, either, and Darryl's dad goes on about that — how their pants have no flies. I bitch about them with Darryl's dad to be polite, and gag on almond squares for his mom. The colony cheats us occasionally, but I'd watch the organic co-op. The guy they send over fidgets around, spills when he's filling the liquid honey bear jars, and seems to have trouble counting change — sketchy as a leaf in the wind.

That description, the leaf in the wind, Darryl came up with. He's good with sayings, but he repeats them too often. He puts the same words in every sentence so if you don't listen closely, it sounds like he's just saying the same thing over and over again. Sometimes he is. Kind of randomly humming and buzzing. His favourite words right now are "fuck" and "sweet". Also "fucking sweet".

We were up on the railway bridge, watching pelicans fly around that man-made waterfall in the river. I thought they were really beautiful, and I was trying to think of a nice way to describe them. I came up with swoopy. Daryl agreed; he said the birds were fucking sweet. He said the water was rippled like silk and was also fucking sweet.

"Yeah," I said, "sweet." I wished I could come up with another word, but Daryl's get stuck in my head.

"D'ya love me?" he asked.

It was eleven o'clock, warm and summery, and the sky was still kind of backlit by the sunset. The pelicans had gone from white with a bit of orange where they reflected the sun off their wings to a kind of pink where they were lit up by a streetlight in the parking lot. It was pretty.

"D'ya love me?" Darryl asked again.

I stared at the pelicans. We were sitting so our legs dangled over the edge of the bridge and he kicked his heels around and asked me again and again, "D'ya love me, d'ya love me, d'ya love me . . . ?"

I barely even heard the train coming because the noise of it blended in with the 'd'ya love me's. And I hate being up there when trains go by. The whole thing shakes and the air smells like blood. It's the metal wheels grinding against the metal railway ties, I know that, but I smell blood and rust. The same smell comes up off of the metal mesh on the honey pasteurizing filters when Darryl is spraying dismembered bees out of them with steaming hot water on his dad's front lawn.

I didn't want to tell Darryl that I was thinking about breaking up with him because of boring sex. Asides from being shallow, it wasn't really true. It was one of the things that felt new the longest, so when it started being the same all the time it made me notice other things about Darryl were always the same. How he's always quoting his dad. And our lives revolving around bees. And Darryl putting words in my mouth and saying 'fucking sweet day' every single night. Not all days are sweet. I used to wake up kind of excited just to be lying beside him. He used to want to be with me even at the end of a day of work, and I didn't used to mind his hands being sticky.

Darryl saw that there were tears on my face after the train and he thought I'd been scared.

"*Tango medio?*" he asked. He knows how to say four or five things in Spanish and he's used them enough that I know a lot of them too. I thought this was, "Were you scared?" Or, "I'm scared?" Or something like that.

"*Besa me, te quiero,*" I said in a bitchy voice, because it was the only other Spanish thing I could remember just then, "kiss me, I desire you." I didn't particularly desire for him to kiss me.

He did though, and then he said, "So, d'ya love me?"

I groaned, and said "*mañana*" which means either tomorrow or morning, and is what Darryl always says to mean, I'm tired, get off me.

My mom told me, before I'd ever even dated anyone, that real love survives passion. That's what she said, and I thought she knew what she was talking about. Two years later she divorced my dad and now she lives on an island making candles. Guess who she buys the wax from. The bees, when we first met, were just Darryl's family thing, now it's all interbred. He brought a drone to Thanksgiving dinner and my cousins watched it nurse on the sweat in the crease of his palm.

"D'ya love me?" Darryl asked again, trying to egg me out of being moody.

"When you don't take me on train bridges to scare me to death," is what I said.

Thanks to Darryl, the smell of candles and craft stores, the smell of my mother, overwhelms me and makes me retch. All those all-natural beeswax products smell like bee supers fresh in from the fields and full of crusting-over honey, wax frames, and dead and dying bees. They bellow smoke into the supers before they pull them apart, to 'calm' the bees down. The bees think there's a fire, and scurry down into the bottom box where their queen and larvae are, but the fumes confuse them and they get stuck in the uncapped honey cells they've spent their whole lives stepping around. Darryl always has one or two whole dead bees and a number of stray bee parts stuck on him when he comes home after work. The bees that almost made it down. It's less than charming to watch him flick them into the shrubs beside our rented doorstep, and his fingers get stuck in my hair when he kisses me because honey sneaks into the cracks in his calluses. It's not that beekeepers don't get stung, it's that they stop reacting.

He got into the shower as soon as we got home, then went straight from there to bed. I thought he'd call me in but he was snoring before I finished putting out the recycling. I called my mom. "Well," she asked, "would you be able to marry him if he wasn't a beekeeper?"

I'd never considered that.

Maybe.

That next morning I asked him if he'd ever thought about doing something other than beekeeping.

"Like what?" he said, which I took as a no, but later he said that he'd thought a lot about being a doctor in high school.

"So, why did you change your mind?" I asked.

He said he'd decided that he'd have to spend too much time in school, and also he might get bored after a while. Colds, flus, and ear infections. Allergies and blood pressure. He said he couldn't take doing the same thing all the time. The next thing he said was that he'd have to restack the Viscount supers on the weekend because a cow had tipped them over again.

Darryl's mom handed me a muffin one day (honey-flavoured) and winked and said that, maybe after I was an official part of the family, she'd share the recipe. The queen, shoving royal jelly into her larva, fattening her successor. If I didn't meet her standards, the next one might, or the next one. Young queens are semi-disposable, most of them get killed off. I had a vision of myself, warped by years of Darryl's mom's baking into a hovering biddy who'd force-feed pastries to the innocent girlfriends of my sons. The only bees that communicate verbally in a hive are the queens, and their language isn't pretty. The official words for it are quacking and tooting. Imagine a farting duck.

I told my dad about this terror during our weekly Tuesday evening phone call, expecting him to laugh and say it would never happen, but he was feeling contemplative and said that it was up to me to determine my fate. This was a funny thing to hear from Dad who has been letting luck and women decide his fate since the day he was born. An elder drone, fattened every summer and kicked out every fall. He's been handed from his mom, to my mom, to a woman named Cheryl, and most recently to Cheryl's sister-in-law, Trudy. I wound the phone cord around my arm and admired the bracelet. He might be a poor source but my dad had a point. I'm not a bee.

I waited until Darryl had proclaimed Tuesday fucking sweet, sighed "*mañana*," and fallen asleep, and then I unwound myself from the sheets and crawled out the foot of the bed. If Darryl really wanted to be with me, he was going to have to come and find me. Enough day-after-dayness. Enough here and nearness too. It was a small cry of defiance, but I moved onto the back veranda and wrapped a blanket around myself in the hammock slung beneath the watchful eyes of one of the green gargoyle candles my mom makes for the hippies. There was a full moon so the porch was well lit up and the gargoyle's waxy candy-heart eyes looked watery and alive. Peering and curious about what I was doing out there.

Not many people know that beeswax is a product of child labour. Newborn bees crawl out of their cells, tidy themselves up, generously push granules of manna into the larval cells around them, and are then compelled by the queen's proletariat to cluster and shimmy until their abdomens sweat slivers of wax. They aren't allowed to stop until their stores are depleted, and it takes about six measures of honey for them to make one measure of wax. It's like liposuctioning the fat off a baby seal. Once they're drained, if they've made it, their first job is to clear away the lifeless husks of the babies who didn't. That's what wax is. Also, it's what their cradles are made of. And what they keep their food in. Being a bee is a very down-to-earth endeavour. And they don't sleep. They hold still at night mostly, but they don't sleep. They can't dream. They never think up other things to do with their wax. They've never seen gargoyles, they could never imagine a dinner candle . . .

I had been planning that, in the morning, Darryl would roll over and fall into an empty spot in the bed (it sags). He'd wake up, wonder where I was, and maybe even panic. When he found me on the back porch he'd frown and swing my hammock a little. He'd know we had to talk about changing things. About giving ourselves some distance from his family and their work. I was, for once, looking forward in a nervous way to morning. I'd say, Look, I love you, but . . .

The phone woke us both up around three a.m. and we met in the hallway just after he'd hung it up.

"Why didn't you get that?" he asked, rubbing his hands up over his face, "fuck!"

"Fuck what?" I asked.

"Dad said Mom — fuck! Did you see where I put my keys — fucking . . ."

His answer descended into grunts while I found his keys and followed him back to the bedroom. He pulled on clothes off the floor and said something I didn't quite catch about cops and death and drove away while I was still looking for clothes to get dressed and go with him.

It really sucks when the (albeit less than continually exciting) love of your life drives away in the middle of the night saying stuff about cops and death, and you don't know why or when he's going to come back. I actually ran out onto the front lawn half-dressed, calling "Wait, Darryl, what?"

I imagined his well-meaning mom dead. I imagined him driving at breakneck pace and hitting something or somebody. It's what bees do, fleeing the hive. They fly straight and will hit anything unfamiliar moved into their way, memory works faster than eyesight in panic mode. Darryl would crash, would get arrested, would drive around disoriented and never come home. I sat in the hammock and cried, wondered, tried calling his parents but had no luck and couldn't guess what that meant.

Darryl's mom didn't only bake, she also spent time promoting the health benefits of honey. She ran a booth at the children's festival where she taught kids and parents that raw comb and royal jelly provide natural antibiotics for developing healthy immune systems. She ran a slightly modified booth at a trade fair in Edmonton promoting raw honey's natural epinephrine. Then she read an article about a woman whose arthritis improved after her husband started a hobby hive in their yard. Then one about how in Russia they're injecting bee venom into the joints of people with gout. She got busy and put up a poster offering therapeutic stingings. Sunset hive tours. Why pass up a side business? Less than three percent of people are allergic to bee stings, most of them only mildly, and most of them know it. Darryl had to co-sign on his mom's bail on manslaughter charges.

I told my Dad that I'd decided to marry Darryl the next Tuesday and he told me not to be 'manipulated by circumstance,' reminding me of the time when I was ten and he told me that I didn't have to play with an obnoxious girl on our street. Feeling sorry for somebody doesn't mean that you have to be friends with them, was what he told me about that girl, Natalie, whose deafness had nothing to do with the fact that she was a bully and a tattler. But I love Darryl. Maybe especially with his mom in jail.

That night when the phone rang and Darryl shot off swearing to rescue his parents from the police, I stood there, half-dressed, on our moonlit front lawn, and I promised that I'd stomach honey-flavoured baking and bitch about Hutterites until I turned into a wrinkled prune if Darryl would get to wherever he was going without hitting a light post. I promised that, if I was allowed to keep him, I'd never retch at a dead bee again. Just then, I couldn't imagine anything nicer than having Darryl with me on the lawn, covered in bee parts, pestering me to say that I loved him. Dancing and shaking and stuck on repeat. I wanted him to come home and spin, "D'ya love me?" again and again and again. He did come back, around five in the morning, groaning, "God I'm tired." I tucked him into our bed and I made myself coffee. I left the new Lee Valley catalogue on the kitchen counter for him and, for the first time, drove out on my own to water the bees.

Sense

ALWYNNE PACKED SIMPLY — THREE TINS OF MAPLE-BAKED beans for three dinners. The heat of her gas stove rose, distorting the bushes hunched against the opposite canyon wall. She twisted the valve and the orange licks narrowed to steel blue flame. She had camped on the barren side of the canyon. By the time she left, her footprints would dimple the sandy gravel plane, but that first night Alwynne was keenly aware of her tracks. She was changing the space as she settled into the campsite she had picked, more or less randomly, among the network of canyons. The stove's heat twisted and charred a blade of grass leaning close and she pressed a few others hastily out of the way with a steel-toed boot.

Dusk had fallen. The sun shone down in the canyons, then bounced. The sand that powdered out of the canyon walls reflected as much as it absorbed. The ground was cool now, leaching warmth from her kneeling shins, but the heat of Alwynne's sunburn increased through the evening, raising angry crescents on the unprotected undersides of her arms and neck. These swaths of skin itched, then stung when rubbed. The burn kept her awake as much as the coyotes did, arriving suddenly to halloo across her campsite. They were on the clifftops, not terribly close, but their voices rose and fell and echoed, laughing and chattering. Fingering burnt skin in the stuffiness of her ancient dome tent, Alwynne drifted bone by bone asleep only when the animals moved on and the night conspired to silence.

She could have camped in a provincial park, or in the guesthouse her clients had paid up for the week, but those options hadn't felt like fieldwork. Alwynne's student summers had been spent almost entirely in the field and she had loved it. The consulting firm provided a social life and a means to pay her mortgage, both necessary — but to be alone, out here, with a rustling sleeping bag and coyotes circling, that was to slip backwards, raw, skinned free.

There had been no friendly lunch or drink with the consortium of researchers from the Geology Department and Natural History museum, only a slightly hostile conference call during which Alwynne's firm was advised, early and repeatedly, that there should be nothing to find. The museum had pre-emptively poled the western face of the valley and tracked ground-penetrating radar along the riverbed that formed the backbone of canyons. They needed an archaeological survey for completeness but a surface find, a midden, wintering site, or medicine wheel, would tangle permits and hold diggers back from the valley's bluff cliffs indefinitely.

The wider area was rich in artifacts of early Plains Culture, tool and weapon fragments were common finds, but the canyons were places where really very little had been left behind. The mini-badlands, sunk into the prairie north of the fossil troves to the south, had been carved by a river system whose source waters were starved by irrigation and civic supply. The riverbed had formed a dry, semi-level road for several generations of ranchers but there was no oral history of permanent or even seasonal First Nations settlement. In winter, the canyons formed an inconvenient snow trap where caches and traplines would have been rapidly buried.

Sense

In summer, the sand was hot and reflective and cliff slumps had a disconcerting tendency to expose enormous bones and teeth.

After a day rumbling a rented ATV up and down the riverbed, it was clear to Alwynne that the canyon's hundred-year history of ranching and paleontology had more than overprinted remnants of human activity over the previous ten thousand years. She found survey pegs and shell casings of assorted vintage, a coil of discarded barbed wire, and a liquor store's quota of bottles and beer cans. She also found several pieces of tooth or bone that looked fossilized, which she pocketed for her nephew Julian, nine and bright, who was very excited about dinosaurs and the fact that Saskatchewan and Alberta lingered — not briefly, but for millennia — at the bottom of a shallow sea.

There was also evidence of quite recent excavation in the canyons, which Alwynne documented duly. There were spade marks at several locations on the western cliff face and two piles of flattish, medium-sized rocks. These had probably been knocked out of the cliff for ditch lining or some other ranching purpose. It would be a pain, to locals, when the canyons turned Crown Land and became policed, but Alwynne was not trying to get anyone in trouble by photographing these disturbed sites. She was thinking of a widely rumoured black market in dinosaur artifacts. If these disturbed sites belonged to the museum, she assumed that they would have been flagged on the map they had provided her, but you never knew. Maybe they were getting a wee head start on their permits, maybe someone else was. Half bored with her task, Alwynne entertained herself imagining criminal paleontologists rooting about in camouflage, clawing for finds in the black of night. Dinosaur poachers catered to a market of eccentric millionaires, devious academics, and enthusiastic pre-teens — they were presumably paid in uncut diamonds, co-authorships, and used comics. Thinking of Julian, Alwynne imagined the pre-teens as precocious, underweight, and male. She had been into plastic gimp bracelets and beading at his age. She matured to hobby silversmithing but retained that early enthusiasm for beads, driven not so much to string them as to find them. There are hobbies you can grow into as well as out of.

Rather than spend her mornings and evenings driving to and from the canyons, Alwynne was camping on site largely so that she could spend time sieving the riverbed — a painstaking, hit-and-miss, but occasionally exhilarating means of isolating some of the most beautiful artifacts of early Plains Culture. Glass beads, tin beads, iron beads, awled porcelain beads, and every now and then a quill.

Light spilled over the canyon wall the next morning and flooded Alwynne's tent. She shook a sleepy stiffness out, swung her arms awake, then lingered over an instant coffee. Dew sparkled around her, reflecting from green grass and leaves. A jackrabbit emerged from a bush, met Alwynne's eyes, then turned to bound to the clifftop in six graceful leaps. Up, up, up it went in perfect silence. This was a promising start to a day during which Alwynne scouted doggedly through mosquito-rich haloes around muddy trickles. Several of these 'springs' had been trenched for cattle and were surrounded by fibrous piles of degrading cowpat. There was little of anthropological interest, but when she returned to her camp, late afternoon, Alwynne found a Coffee Crisp wrapper.

In the grey strip of gravel where she parked the ATV, the yellow candy wrapper stood out like flagging. On close inspection, it was held aloft by a coil of shit. Coyote sized. To avoid stepping in this, Alwynne scooped the poop into a bag of garbage she was packing out, frowning suspiciously at the chocolate wrapper. Coyotes range far, but ever an evidence-based scientist, Alwynne found herself wondering how long it took them to process their food.

The answer would have been at her fingertips online, but she'd left her phone behind, not expecting coverage. NO TRESSPASSING signs were clear and abundant but new. It was possible that the coyote had obtained the chocolate wrapper from someone willing to ignore them, which would mean that Alwynne was not as alone in the canyons as she had assumed. She would have heard a car in the last day-and-a-half, probably, but as recently as the morning before there could have been other visitors. Dark and handsome traders in dinosaur bones, perhaps.

After a second day of unprofitable surveying, Alwynne considered packing the fieldwork in. There were three more marked sites on her GPS, sheltered areas likely to have been camped in and unlikely to flood, but she wasn't expecting to find anything important. Unless she sieved. She had seen a place where a miniature flood plain had sorted the sediment by grain size. Beads would settle amongst coarse sand. The idea of a cool evening, sun setting to the rhythmic grating of her sieves (she had an automated oscillator that plugged into the power port on the ATV) was appealing. A look at herself in the ATV's side mirror, her neck lobster red yet sliced through by strips of white that marked the folds of a slight double chin, decided it. She was unfit for civilization and had two more cans of beans awaiting.

Sieving on her own time in an as-yet-unpermitted area, Alwynne would not have needed to report any beads that she found. Although she would, for completeness. And out of stubbornness. The boss had seen no need to take sieves on a cursory survey, but all parties would later admit that the two milky glass beads she isolated after three hours of sieving were the perfect find. Evidence that real efforts had been made to connect with the area's anthropological history, but nothing to hold up a backhoe. They were mundane artifacts, a non-expert might have taken them for plastic. They had been crizzled, made opaque by structural changes in the aging glass. Alwynne pictured them new — bright, clear, and faintly silver moons set against dark tanned leather, treasures worth bartering for. She teased them from equi-sized sand and bagged them as prizes. She crawled into her tent smiling, itching, and slightly bloated after a second, less nostalgic meal of maple beans.

She woke past midnight, starting at a yelp that she took, initially, for coyote. The replying hoot sounded much closer than the clifftops. Coyotes don't swear or protest. Or bang. She heard popping sounds that could be fireworks or guns. More swearing, a pause, and an elated whoop. A laugh. Picturing cowboys with guns, Alwynne hurried herself into clothes, but the canyon fell suddenly silent. Ammo wasted? Firecrackers spent? Alwynne paused, half in and half out of her dome tent, and heard a series of thuds. Muted crashes as slumping earth and gravel tripped down the canyon wall. They seemed to be destabilizing the cliffs. Throwing rocks maybe? It carried on for five or ten minutes before she heard a vehicle start. A door slam. Very close by, maybe two city blocks. She drew herself upright and stood just in time to catch a sweep of headlights across the opposite canyon wall. Red tail lights bounced away at a speed that could only be considered dangerous on a semi-level riverbed. If they'd come farther up the riverbed they might have hit her ATV. Or swerved around it and crushed her in her tent. As insurance, Alwynne set two lit flashlights upright in the gravel, but the rest of the night was very quiet. The coyotes, she supposed, had been spooked into silence too.

That morning, Alwynne walked her instant coffee towards a swerve of fresh tire marks. The drunken farm boys had made what could only be called a mess of the cliff. A large section was disturbed, though if she hadn't overheard the rock hurling Alwynne might have taken it for a natural slide. The cliff edges, especially on the eastern side, were unstable. It was hard to tell what in the canyon was geological and what had been rearranged by a hundred years of quarrying and vandalism. She supposed that pot shooting and rock throwing were harmless, really. They probably *were* looking for dinosaurs, if not for black marketeering then simply to grasp their share of notoriety after the publicity around the *T. Rex* discovered by teenagers fishing in the Crowsnest Pass. The only danger would have been if they had fired their crackers/guns in her direction, because they really had been fairly close. It seemed that the canyon was less isolated than she had taken it to be, which left Alwynne feeling self-conscious about the previous evening. Her T-shirt had been bothering her sunburnt skin so she'd sieved topless, stripped to her bra. A red neckline was nothing compared to double Cs racked up in that hefty, flesh-toned, and undoubtedly sweat-stained support.

Alwynne had the option of leaving that morning, surveying the last few sites and leaving in the afternoon, or surveying the last few sites and spending another evening sieving. If it weren't for the beads, she would have left. They rolled in their Ziploc like tiny promises. The day stretched out again, tripping into the canyon's sudden dusk, for there was no lingering sunset in the canyon. Shadow swept over the cliff and Alwynne was caught stacking her sieves and deliberating a dark drive out. If it hadn't been for the car the night before, she would have left, driving slowly and carefully with the ATV's floodlights pointed ahead. But the possibility of a collision with probably harmless but drunk and armed men was fresh in her mind. She had sieved for three hours and found only one irregular piece of glass, which was more likely a bottle fragment than a bead.

Several times during the sieving, Alwynne had thought she heard footsteps but the sound, or impression, disappeared when she turned the oscillator off to listen. It could easily have been animals, deer or even rabbits. Stacking the sieves, Alwynne listened again, and heard nothing, but smelled something vaguely marine. Salt, water, and decaying plants. Something intangible which seemed to have been shaken out of the sand with her fragment of glass.

The wind, which had been barely noticeable during her three days outside, picked up that evening, buffeting the bushes across from her campsite. Alwynne imagined the coyotes up on the flat, streaming past single file, noses pointed into the wind. Despite the blustery weather, she expected another car, and set two flashlights upright outside her tent. She was more afraid of being shot at or run over than she was of talking to young men. She'd had, often to her dismay, a calming, big-sisterly sort of influence on the male species since her teens. She came across as matronly and knew she could talk them down if they came up to her tent. She could even offer them a drink, since she hadn't touched the flask of whisky she always carried out to the field. The previous two nights she hadn't felt in need of anything other than silence, and tonight she wanted to be clear headed. To hear things coming, cars or predators. Coyotes rarely attack, but they too, might be drawn to her lights.

This was the time, really, when Alwynne should have used the satellite phone. If not to call a conservation officer to give a head's up as to what had been going on, then at least to call a friend. Talking would have settled her. She felt afraid, and irritated with herself for it. She caught herself wondering about being able to spot a black animal in the dark. Found herself staring at the animal-eye reflections of her flashlight on the undersides of waxy, wind-bustled leaves. Those spaced like eyes would dip and lurk, before dancing inevitably apart. Coming to the field alone now felt less freeing than foolish. Alwynne believed in instincts — trusting her subconscious to deal more completely with subtle sensory input than her sentient mind. Yet she felt irrational, bothered that she couldn't drop her guard and enjoy a third, rare night of freedom.

Sense

What Alwynne did was pull out stickers and label her tiny finds. She drew fishing line through the little white beads, tagged them, and nested them individually in plastic vials with wads of cotton. They had tumbled perhaps miles downstream, worked free from a discarded garment, or spilled from a pouch of ornaments. They had travelled. The GPS coordinates of their capture meant nothing to them, but would become their names. Alwynne pulled out the fragments she had collected for Julian and labelled them with the same care. Then she went through her digital camera's archive, deleting out-of-focus shots and making detailed notes on the rest of the pictures. When the wind haranguing her tent fly got too distracting, she crawled inside to wait for a car's rumble down the gravel incline.

Nestled in her sleeping bag, Alwynne relived her last trip to a beading store, where crates of beads, every size and colour and material, had overwhelmed to the point that she lost enthusiasm for buying anything. Then she imagined wiring the two crizzled beads on a pendant, a mobius strip of silver, with narrowings in the ribbon, one on each loop. Calmed, and dreamier, she imagined the boys coming up the canyon towards her tent. She felt increasingly confident, as she planned a casual greeting and invitation to drink, that they would not come back. When she got up for a midnight pee she turned the flashlights off, sick of the lights shining into her tent.

They came very early in the morning. It was still dark in the canyon but the sky was a pre-dawn grey. Alwynne heard a yell, slightly farther away than the night before.

"This one ain't no lightweight!" A chain of pops. A muted thud. Another, and then the clunk and echo of slumping gravel. A shout she could only describe as giddy and gleeful. Wildly human. She found herself in a squat, laughing. She had been more afraid without them than she was now that they were, it seemed, just around the nearest bend in the riverbed. The distance gave her time to dress. To boil water. To make coffee. The boys kept throwing rocks. She wondered if it had been firecrackers after all, the night before, or if they'd been setting up bottles.

"Shit move!"

"They're fucking bouncing, I can't help it!"

A bruise or two might get them over the thrill. They definitely lacked the romance of her palaeontological poacher, slipping out of field dust into a tuxedo and backroom lounge. Apparently throwing rocks was more these guys' thing. They were high on it, and after Alwynne heard what she thought sounded like a girl's laugh, she quit worrying. They were showing off. The sun was minutes away from the cliff's edge when their doors slammed and the engines, of maybe two vehicles this time, revved up and away.

There are things that feel important, but aren't understood, and method can bring these things meaning. Subtle variations in flint tools, plotted with care, reveal migration paths and orders of tribal contact. Science can move through its methods, a dreaming mind connecting images in narrative. And ceremony can do the same. The ritualized drudgery of sieving offering glimpses of a culture filled with hope, enriched by beauty. A nomadic people bound to transportable art which, disassembled, continued to travel, settling only in shifting sand.

Over her coffee that morning, Alwynne mulled over the fact that, if you were in a mood to throw rocks, the act itself — the efforts of lifting and hurling — could be infused with meaning. A rich, ripe ceremony. The young had lost, with agnosticism and modernity, a certain depth of respect for the world, that was true. Alwynne wondered how much this had to do with the loss of predators. Raised in a society coddled by technology, why shouldn't youth dare the night? Why shouldn't they embrace their ancestors' fears as their playground? Between times, a wildness that freed could endanger, and a canyon that protected could also corner. Those impressions would only have been stronger ten thousand years ago when the river pooled in ochre beds, sabre tooths roamed, and monsters clawed their way out of the canyon walls.

Alwynne had partaken of something ancient in the night and felt compelled to acknowledge it. She picked larger pebbles out of the gravel and stacked them while sipping a watery mug of instant oatmeal. She piled them into a pyramid, about a foot high, to make their placement obvious. Wind, rain, or tires would knock them over in short order, but for now, stacking them was ceremony. An honouring of wildness in a tire-tracked space, the creation of a relict that, casting its small triangular shadow, looked unexpectedly monumental. This did not feel entirely out of place — she was in a graveyard of sorts, after all.

Julian's endearing excitement with dinosaurs aside, Alwynne found fossils somewhat morbid. Human burials tend to be respect-fully arranged, even in cannibalistic circumstances, but dinosaurs and the like had more often than not been shredded by predators and scattered by decay. Excepting 'pristine' finds, most of their lizardly hard parts were scattered, then sorted by the forces of currents and waves, just as Alwynne's beads had been. There was a compulsive insistence in sixty-five million years of sorting At some locations it produced fossil suites preset for classification, sized for science's appraisal as tidily as wood screws in a hardware store. Beads, bin six, row four. Gastroliths, bin seven, row three. Have you got any teeth in stock?

At the Green Moon guesthouse, Alwynne planted herself in the cruddy tin shower and dealt with her sunburn. She peeled unsightly coins of weathered skin from what was really just barely a double chin. A similar situation had rendered her underarms offensively itchy. Before going public, she scrubbed herself raw, then dressed gingerly in clean clothes. Alwynne followed a gravel path to the guesthouse's restaurant trailer where she ordered chicken strips and fries so that she could eat with one hand. With the other, she began form filling on her laptop, her attention divided between writing, eating, and watching the news on a TV behind the till. The weather was expected to turn, with rain forecast for the rest of July. Alwynne dripped buffalo dipping sauce down her wrist and, finding the napkin dispenser empty, gave it a surreptitious lick. A politician she recognized had been indicted on charges of impaired driving. And there was a missing twenty-year-old, last seen at a gas station nearby. The brief cameo showed a young Asian man grinning beside a rhododendron, and Alwynne's attention was caught by the fuchsia flowers, rather than the boy's pose or the details of his face. There was brief mention of other young men, missing since the previous March, and of the infiltration of Asian-Pacific gangs into the Alberta drug scene. Throwing rocks, shooting bottles, even shooting coyotes, maybe these weren't such dangerous activities after all. Alwynne filled in her forms, emailed them to the boss, and copied them to the summer student who, for the sake of a wedding, had backed out of accompanying her. Alwynne was giving the all-clear to their clients. As she walked back to her room, she opened a hand to the first spatters of rain.

The twenty-year old was discovered by an undergraduate paleontology student during an intersession field trip the following spring. Three other bodies were sniffed out by cadaver dogs after the canyon was cordoned off. The young dead had bowed to the weights of sand and gravel and their decay opened gaps in the slumped cliffs of the eastern canyon wall. The RCMP encouraged the public to come forward. They wanted any possible information but Alwynne had deleted the images and their coordinates from her camera months before. She had the coordinates of her sieving sites, the tagnames of her crizzled beads, but these had no connection to those young lives. She hadn't included images of the cairns in her report. Those strangely stacked piles of stone had seemed irrelevant, in the end, and she couldn't remember whether they had struck her as recent or relict. She tried to recreate the conversation, the yells she had overheard — but there had been no names, nothing that stuck. The sound had been unbridled, loose in the night. Had she been further down the canyon she might have mistaken them for coyotes, moondrunk, yelping at the sky. What could she have added to the investigation? That the canyons were busy places. That she had been afraid. That a girl laughed and she took that for proof of safety and maybe it was.

A live flame will start

I THINK SOMETIMES I MAY HAVE died halfway. When I wake up in the closet, in the kitchen, on the cement floor of the basement, I don't remember arriving. Was I walking towards John? Or was I with him somewhere, in some alternate place, together the way we were before? I do very normal things in my sleep — I start loads of laundry, I pull books from the shelves, I put the kettle on the stove and wake up when it starts to whistle. Do we do such ordinary things when we are dead?

I wake to the street being quiet and the house being dark — the fridge hums, the moon shines down. The furnace sighs off and surges on, but I keep the bedroom window that careful inch open, so his dreams can breathe.

His mother insisted on the urn. A squat, copper thing. I dreamt that John stole it from its shelf in the columbarium and brought it to me. He woke me up, a hand on my back, and held it towards me, grinning.

It is the same grin that taught me about love and forgiveness. Hope. Odd pieces of hope. John once found a transparent newt and carried it home, opening his hand to show me. He grinned when I gasped at it, such a small and fragile thing. It was meant to live on the mossy side of trees because it couldn't take the sun, so we kept it for a week in the bathroom, where the air is humid and it's dark enough. But John couldn't get it to eat. He offered it everything from bugs to worms to little bits of hamburger. In the end, we took it back to the woods where it could live properly beside a mushroom-ringed tree. It slipped from John's palm, twisted in the moss, and blinked.

I imagine it thought that John's hand was a bird, his fingers a soft beak, and our bathroom a belly, digesting it slowly. It didn't expect to be let go.

I think sometimes that I am halfway gone with John. Half-digested by his grin. I don't feel very well, I have slipped beyond missing him, beyond grieving. When I sleep, I wake up where I least expect to be. In the shower with my pajamas on and a squirt of shampoo in my hand, awakened, I imagine, by the noisy squeeze of air out of the shampoo bottle. Am I leaving the bed on purpose, avoiding his absence even in my sleep? Or am I going somewhere with him? I long to believe in a dream space where we are together and where, just as I wake, he is wondering, where did she go? She was just here. Just putting the kettle on for me, just reading in that chair.

His mother told me, wincing, that she would understand if I wanted to date another man.

I dreamt that John and I took the urn to a seashore, rocky and weedy, and threw his ashes in. They flew to the open mouths of anemones that sucked greedily on our fingertips, to the mouths of the spotted rockfish whose Latin name he knew but couldn't remember. "Ahhh," he said, rapping his fingers against his forehead. Forgetting.

I'm fine awake — sad, a little. Tired. I go to work and read pages without absorbing a thing. I've started editing, instead of writing — the other half of my brain seems to be missing, wandering somewhere. My mother told me that it was time for me to try to get out a bit. Climb out of my head. Start to have a life again. My sister, Anne, brought me a cat, and signed us up for a clay class.

Cats and pottery. Is this how we mourn? I watch the cat at the window, chattering for birds. I named him Judith, feeling cruel. I dreamt of taking him to John at the beach. I tried to make light of the fact that Anne had tried to replace him with a cat. John smiled, stroked poor Judith, who was rescued by the SPCA from a storm drain and has half a tail, and whispered "You need to deal gently with mammals." So, death is past the jealousies of life, is wiser.

Anne and I made mugs, saucers, and hand-pressed bowls. We traded the bowls, dimpled by each other's fingertips, glaze pooled in the pads. I put Judith's food in my sister's creation, and had to laugh at his purr. I laughed. I wondered if I was waking finally. If, leaning on my sister, on this half-tailed cat, I could slide back to a time before John — a time when he was no one but the boy everyone knew wore homemade jeans, the one I barely knew the size or shape of. A time when I was in one piece without him. The instructor suggested that we should look at art and photography books at the library to find an idea for a final project. And I found a book. Or the book found me. A sculptor tied a scarf around his eyes for six months and sculpted his wife by feel alone.

A live flame will start

For the last night of our class we are asked to invite guests to view our work on display, one night only, in the little gallery fronting the clay studio. A step behind Anne, my niece has her first sip of wine, her first nibble of blue cheese.

"How nice," my mother whispers, placing a hand on my shoulder, "a little lizard."

Its skin fakes translucence with a pearly glaze; its eyes are closed in sleep. She expected a vase like my sister's. My newt sleeps, on display between plates, sculpted nudes, wine chalices, and a collection of avant-garde kitchen tiles. My mother is worried about the way that I cling to my paper plate.

When we wrap our pieces to take them home, I explain to our instructor that it is a Pacific Coast Newt. I explain how, in reality, its organs would show through its skin as small grey shadows. How it eats insects that only live in moss and how its limbs are made of cartilage and can grow back. How you can see its vertebrae when John holds it up to the fluorescent bathroom light.

Source Notes

The opening quotation comes from the book, *Conversations with Chinua Achebe*, by Chinua Achebe and Bernth Lindfors, 1997. Jackson, MS: University Press of Mississippi, p. 80.

The Rilke poetry quoted in Angela and Dean's notes in the story "Open Land" is extracted from a translation of Rainer Maria Rilke's [1875-1926] "Aus Einer Sturmnacht" in *Rilke; selected poems*, translated by C.F. MacIntyre, 1940. Los Angeles, CA: University of California Press, p. 55.

The book referenced at the beginning of the story *"Tango Medio"* is *Sex Is a 13-Letter Word*, by Carolyn Chernenkoff & William Chernenkoff, 1995. Regina: Centax Books.

Translations of the Spanish phrases in this story are as follows:
   Tango Medio — tango (dance) medio (medium, median, halfway) — 'meet me half way'.
   Besa me, te quiero — 'kiss me, I love you'.
   mañana — 'tomorrow', or 'in the morning'.

The title of the story "A live flame will start" is drawn from the poem "To Bring the Dead to Life" by Robert Graves [1895–1985]: To bring the dead to life / Is no great magic. / Few are wholly dead: / Blow on a dead man's embers / And a live flame will start.

Previous Appearances

"Carys," "Nògha," and "Sense": Jarman, M.A., ed. *Coming Attractions 11* (ed.). Ottawa: Oberon Press, 2011, 40–78.

"Carys": *EVENT Magazine* (40th Year Anniversary issue) 40.2 (2011).

"Nògha": *Prairiefire* 30.4 (2010).

"Frames": Davis, C., M.W. Senechal, and J. Zwicky, eds. *The Shape of Content: An Anthology of Creative Writing in Mathematics and Science* (). Natick, MS: A.K. Peters Publishing, 2008, 25–26.

"The Jasmine Springs Road": *The Danforth Review* 24 (2008).

"A live flame will start": *Grain Magazine* 32.3 (2005).

"Tell" (published as "Five Pillars"): *Transition Magazine* 5 (2003).

The story "Mandala" was published as "mandala" in *enRoute Magazine* (May 2002).

Sandy Bonny has been publishing her short fiction since 2002, when her story "mandala" received second place in the CBC Literary Awards.